HIS
MILLION-DOLLAR
MARRIAGE
PROPOSAL

JENNIFER HAYWARD

MILLS & BOON

First Published in Great Britain 2018
by Mills & Boon, an imprint of HarperCollins*Publishers*
1 London Bridge Street, London, SE1 9GF

© 2018 Jennifer Hayward

ISBN: 978-0-263-93459-5

MIX
Paper from
responsible sources
FSC® C007454

This book is produced from independently certified FSC™ paper
to ensure responsible forest management.
For more information visit www.harpercollins.co.uk/green.

Printed and bound in Spain
by CPI, Barcelona

For Mary Sullivan and Stefanie London,
my walking partners and brainstormers extraordinaire.
Thank you for being such amazing writers and women!
Our Wed writing craft chats make my week.

CHAPTER ONE

THURSDAY NIGHT DRINKS at Di Fiore's had been a weekly ritual for Lazzero Di Fiore and his brothers ever since Lazzero and his younger brother, Santo, had parlayed a dream of creating the world's hottest athletic wear into a reality at a tiny table near the back as students at Columbia University.

The jagged slash of red fire, the logo they had scratched into the thick mahogany tabletop to represent the high-octane Supersonic brand, now graced the finely tuned bodies of some of the world's highest paid athletes, a visibility which had, in turn, made the brand a household name.

Unfortunately, Lazzero conceded blackly as he wound his way through the crowd in the packed, buzzing, European-style sports bar he and Santo ran in midtown Manhattan, success had also meant their personal lives had become public fodder. A fact of life he normally took in stride. The breech of his inner sanctum, however, had been the final straw.

He absorbed the show of feminine leg on display on what was supposed to be Triple-Play Thursdays—a ritual for Manhattan baseball fans. Inhaled the cloud of expensive perfume in the air, thick enough to take down a lesser man. *This* was all *her* doing. He'd like to strangle her.

"This is turning into a three-ring circus," he muttered, sliding into a chair at the table already occupied by his brothers, Santo and Nico.

"Because the city's most talked-about gossip columnist chose to make us number two on her most-wanted bachelor list?" Santo, elegant in black Hugo Boss, cocked a brow. "If we sue, it'd have to be for finishing behind Barnaby Alexander. He puts his dates to sleep recounting his billions. I find it highly insulting."

"Old money," Nico supplied helpfully. "She had to mix it up a bit."

Lazzero eyed his elder brother, who was probably thanking his lucky stars he'd taken himself off the market with his recent engagement to Chloe, with whom he ran Evolution—one of the world's most successful cosmetic companies. "I'm glad you're finding this amusing," he growled.

Nico shrugged. "You would too if you were in the middle of *my* three-ring circus. Why I ever agreed to a Christmas wedding is beyond me."

Lazzero couldn't muster an ounce of sympathy, because the entire concept of marriage was insanity to him.

"*Show it* to me," he demanded, glaring at Santo.

Santo slid the offending magazine across the table, his attention captured by a glamorous-looking blonde staring unashamedly at him from the bar. Loosening his tie, he sat back in his chair and gave her a thorough once-over. "Not bad at all."

Utterly Santo's type. She looked ready for anything.

Lazzero fixed his smoldering attention on the list of New York's most eligible bachelors as selected by Samara Jones of *Entertainment Buzz*. A follow-up to her earlier piece that had declared the "Summer Lover" the year's hottest trend, the article, cheekily entitled "The Summer Shag" in a nod to Jones's British heritage, featured her top twenty bachelors with which to fulfill that seasonal pursuit.

Lazzero scanned the list, his perusal sliding to a halt at entry number two:

Since they're gorgeous and run the most popular athletic-wear company on the planet—Lazzero and Santo Di Fiore clock in at number two. Young, rich and powerful, they are without a doubt the most delicious double dose of testosterone in Manhattan. Find them at Di Fiore's on Thursday nights, where they still run their weekly strategy sessions from the corner table where it all started.

Lazzero threw the magazine on the table, a look of disgust claiming his face. "You do realize that *this*," he said, waving a hand around them, "is never going to be ours again?"

"Relax," Santo drawled, eyes now locked with the sophisticated blonde who couldn't take her eyes off his equally glamorous profile. "Give it a few weeks and it'll die down."

"Or not."

Santo shifted his attention back to the table. "What's got you so twisted in a knot?" he queried. "It can't be *that*," he said, inclining his head toward the magazine. "You've been off for weeks."

Lazzero blew out a breath and sat back in his chair. "Gianni Casale," he said flatly. "I had a call with him this afternoon. He isn't biting on the licensing deal. He's mired in red ink, knows his brand has lost its luster, knows we're eating his lunch, and still he won't admit he needs this partnership."

Which was a problem given Lazzero had forecast Supersonic would be the number two sportswear company in the world by the end of the following year, a promise his influential backers were banking on. Which meant acquiring Gianni Casale's legendary Fiammata running shoe technology, Volare, was his top priority.

Santo pointed his glass at him. "Let's be honest here. The *real* problem with Casale is that he hates your guts."

Lazzero blinked. "*Hate* is a strong word."

"Not when you used to date his wife. Everyone knows Carolina married Gianni on the rebound from you, his bank balance a salve for her wounded heart. She makes it clear every time you're in a room together. She's still in love with you, Laz, her marriage is on the rocks and Casale is afraid he can't hold her. *That's* our problem."

Guilt gnawed at his insides. He'd told Carolina he would never commit—that he just didn't have it in him. The truth, given his parents' disastrous, toxic wreck of a marriage he'd sworn never to repeat. And she'd been fine with it, until all of a sudden, a couple of months into their relationship, she'd grown far too comfortable with his penthouse key, showing up uninvited to cook him dinner after a trip to Asia— a skill he hadn't even known she'd possessed.

Maybe he'd ignored one too many warning signs, had been so wrapped up in his work and insane travel schedule he hadn't called it off soon enough, but he'd made it a clean break when he had.

"Gianni cannot possibly be making this personal," he grated. "This is a fifty-million-dollar deal. It would be the height of stupidity."

"He wouldn't be the first man to let his pride get in his way," Santo observed drily. He arched a brow. "You want to solve your problem? Come play in La Coppa Estiva next week. Gianni is playing. Bring a beautiful woman with you to convince him you are off the market and use the unfettered access to him to talk him straight."

Lazzero considered his jam-packed schedule. "I don't have time to come to Milan," he dismissed. "While you're off gallivanting around Italy, wooing your celebrities, someone needs to steer the ship."

Santo eyed him. "*Gallivanting?* Do you have any idea

how much work it is to coordinate a charity game at this level? I want to shoot myself by the end of it."

Lazzero held up a hand. "Okay, I take it back. You are brilliant, you know you are."

La Coppa Estiva, a charity soccer game played in football-crazy Milan, was sponsored by a handful of the most popular brands in the world, including both Supersonic and Fiammata. The biggest names in the business played in the game as well as sponsors and their partners, which made for a logistical nightmare of huge egos and impossible demands. It was only because of his skill managing such a circus that Santo had been named chairman for the second year in a row.

Lazzero exhaled. Took a pull of his beer. Santo was right—he should go. La Coppa Estiva was the only event in the foreseeable future he would get any access to Gianni. "I'll make it work," he conceded, "but I have no idea who I'd take."

"Says the man with an address book full of the most beautiful women in New York," Nico countered drily.

Lazzero shrugged. "I'm too damn busy to date."

"How about a *summer shag*?" Santo directed a pointed look at the strategically placed females around the room. "Apparently, they're all the rage. According to Samara Jones, you keep them around until you've finished the last events in the Hamptons, then say arrivederci after Labor Day. It's ideal, *perfect* actually. It might even put you in a better mood."

"Excellent idea," Nico drawled. "I like it a lot. Particularly the part where we recover his good humor."

Lazzero was not amused. Acquiring himself a temporary girlfriend was the last thing he had the bandwidth for right now. But if that's what it took to convince Gianni he was of no threat to him, then that's what he would do.

Making that choice from the flock of ambitious types

presently hunting him and ending up in Samara Jones's column, however, was not an option. What he needed was an utterly discrete, trustworthy woman who would take this on as the business arrangement it would be and wouldn't expect anything more from him when it was done.

Surely that couldn't be too hard to find?

Friday mornings at the Daily Grind on the Upper West Side were a nonstop marathon. Students from nearby Columbia University, attracted by its urban cool vibe, drifted in like sleepy, rumpled sheep, sprawling across the leather sofas with their coffee, while the slick-suited urban warriors who lived in the area dashed in on the way to the office, desperate for a fix before that dreaded early meeting.

Today, however, had tested the limits of even coolheaded barista Chiara Ferrante's even-keeled disposition. It might have been the expensive suit who'd just rolled up to the counter, a set of Porsche keys dangling from his fingertips, a cell phone glued to his ear, and ordered a grande, half-caff soy latte at exactly 120 degrees, *no more, no less*, on the heels of half a dozen such ridiculous orders.

You need this job, Chiara. Now more than ever. Suck it up and just do it.

She took a deep, Zen-inducing breath and cleared the lineup with ruthless efficiency, dispatching the walking Gucci billboard with a 119-degree latte—a minor act of rebellion she couldn't resist. A brief lull ensuing, she turned to take inventory of the coffee bar on the back wall before the next wave hit.

"You okay?" Kat, her fellow barista and roommate asked, as she replenished the stack of take-out cups. "You seem off today."

Chiara gathered up the empty carafes and set them in the sink. "The bank turned down my father's request for a loan. It hasn't been a good morning."

Kat's face fell. "Oh, God. I'm sorry. I know it's been hard for him to make a go of it lately. Are there any other banks he can try?"

"That was the last." Chiara bit her lip. "Maybe Todd can give me some more shifts."

"And turn you into the walking dead? You've been working double shifts for months, Chiara. You're going to fall flat on your face." Kat leaned a hip against the bar. "What you need," she said decisively, "is a rich man. It would solve all your problems. They're constantly propositioning you and yet you never take them up on their offers."

Because the one time she had, he'd shattered her heart into pieces.

"I'm not interested in a rich man," she said flatly. "They come in here in their beautiful suits, drunk on their power, thinking their money gives them license to do anything they like. It's all a big game to them, the way they play with women."

Kat flashed her an amused look. "That's an awfully big generalization don't you think?"

Chiara folded her arms over her chest. "Bonnie, Sivi and Tara went out the other night to Tempesta Di Fuoco, Stefan Bianco's place in Chelsea. They're sitting at the bar when this group of investment bankers starts chatting them up. Bonnie's thrilled when *Phil* asks her out for dinner at Lido. She goes home early because she's opening here in the morning. Sivi and Tara stay." She lifted a brow. "What does *Phil* do? He asks Sivi out to lunch."

"Pig," Kat agreed, making a face. "But you can't paint all men with the same brush."

"Not all men. *Them*. The suit," Chiara declared scathingly, "may change, but the man inside it doesn't."

"I'm afraid I have to disagree," a deep, lightly accented voice intoned, rippling a reactionary path down her spine. "It would be a shame for *Phil* to give us all a bad name."

Chiara froze. Turned around slowly, her hands gripping the marble. Absorbed the tall, dark male leaning indolently against the counter near the silver bell she wished fervently he'd rung. Clad in a silver Tom Ford suit that set off his swarthy skin to perfection, Lazzero Di Fiore was beautiful in a predatory, hawk-like way—oozing an overt sex appeal that short-circuited the synapses in her brain.

The deadpan expression on his striking face indicated he'd heard every last word of her ill-advised speech. "I—" she croaked, utterly unsure of what to say "—you should have rung the bell."

"And missed your fascinatingly candid appraisal of Manhattan's finest?" His sensual mouth twisted. "Not for the world. Although I do wonder if I could have an espresso to fuel my *overinflated ego*? I have a report I need to review for a big hotshot meeting in exactly fifty minutes."

Kat made a sound at the back of her throat. Chiara's cheeks flamed. "Of course," she mumbled. "It's on the house."

On the house. Oh, my God. Chiara unlocked her frozen knees as Lazzero strode off to find a table near the window. Chitchatting with Lazzero when he came in in the mornings was par for the course. Insulting the regulars and losing her job was not.

Amused rather than insulted by the normally composed barista's diatribe, Lazzero ensconced himself at a table near the windows and pulled out his report. Given his cynical attitude of late, it was refreshing to discover not all women in Manhattan were bounty hunters intent on razing his pockets.

It was also, he conceded, fascinating insight into the ultracool Chiara and what lay beneath those impenetrable layers of hers. He'd watched so many men crash and burn in their attempts to scale those defences over the past year he'd been coming here, he could have fashioned a graveyard out of their pitiful efforts. But now, it all made sense. She had been burned and burned badly by a man with power and influence and she wasn't ever going there again.

None of which, he admitted, flipping open the report on the Italian fashion market his team had prepared, was helping him nail his strategy for winning Gianni Casale over at La Coppa Estiva. The fifty-page report he needed to inhale might. As for a woman to take to Milan to satisfy Gianni's territorial nature? He was coming up blank.

He'd gone through his entire contact list last night in an effort to find a woman who would be appropriate for the business arrangement he had in mind, but none of them was right for the job. All of his ex-girlfriends would interpret the invitation in entirely the wrong light. Ask someone new and she would do the same. And since he had no interest of any kind in a relationship—summer shag or otherwise—that was out too.

Chiara broke his train of thought as she arrived with his espresso. Bottom lip caught between her teeth, a frown pleating her brow, she seemed to be searching for something to say. Then, clearly changing her mind, she reached jerkily for one of the cups on her tray. The steaming dark brew sloshed precariously close to the sides, his expensive suit a potential target. Lazzero reached up to take it from her before she dumped it all over him, his fingers brushing against hers as he did.

A sizzling electrical pulse traveled from her fingers through his, unfurling a curl of heat beneath his skin. Their gazes collided. *Held.* He watched her pupils flare in reaction—her beautiful eyes darkening to a deep, lagoon green.

It was nothing new. They'd been dancing around this particular attraction for weeks, *months.* He, because he was a creature of habit, and destroying his morning routine when it all went south hadn't appealed. She, apparently because he was one of the last men on earth she wanted to date.

Teeth sinking deeper into that lush, delectable lower lip, her long, dark lashes came down to veil her expression. "Enjoy your coffee," she murmured, taking a step back and continuing on her way.

Lazzero sat back in his chair, absorbing the pulse of attraction that zigzagged through him. He didn't remember the last time he'd felt it—felt *anything* beyond the adrenaline that came with closing a big deal and even that was losing its effect on him. That it would be the untouchable enigma that was Chiara who inspired it was an irony that didn't escape him.

He watched her deliver an espresso to an old Italian guy a couple of tables away. At least sixty with a shock of white hair and weathered olive skin, the Italian flirted outrageously with her in his native language, making her smile and wiping the pinched, distracted look from her face.

She was more than pretty when she smiled, he acknowledged. The type of woman who needed no makeup at all to look beautiful with her flawless skin and amazing green eyes. Not to mention her very Italian curves presently holding poor Claudio riveted. With the right clothes and the raw edges smoothed out, she might even be stunning.

And she spoke Italian.

She was perfect, it dawned on him. Smart, gorgeous and clearly not interested in him or his money. She did, however, need to help her father. *He* needed a beautiful woman on his arm to take to Italy who would allow him to focus on the job at hand. One who would have no expectations about the relationship when it was over.

For the price of a couple of pieces of expensive jewelry, what he'd undoubtedly have to fork out for any woman he invited to go with him, he could solve both their problems.

He lifted the espresso to his mouth with a satisfied twist

of his lips and took a sip. Nearly spit it out. Chiara looked over at him from where she stood chatting with Claudio. "What's wrong?"

"Sugar." He grimaced and pushed the cup away. "Since when did I ever take sugar?"

"Oh, God." She pressed a hand to her mouth. "It's Claudio that takes sugar." She bustled over to retrieve his cup. "I'm sorry," she murmured. "I'm so distracted today. I'll fix it."

Lazzero waved her into the chair opposite him when she returned. "Sit."

Chiara gave him a wary look. She'd started to apologize a few minutes ago, then stopped because she'd meant every word she'd said and Lazzero Di Fiore was the worst offender of them all when it came to the broken hearts he'd left strewn across Manhattan. Avoiding her attraction to him *was* the right strategy.

She crossed one ankle over the other, her fingers tightening around her tray. "I should get back to work."

"Five minutes," Lazzero countered. "I have something I want to discuss with you."

Something he wanted to discuss with her? A glance at the bar revealed Kat had the couple of customers well in hand. Utterly against her better judgment, she set her tray down and slid into the chair opposite Lazzero.

The silver-gray suit and crisp, tailored white shirt set off his olive skin and toned muscular physique to perfection. He looked so gorgeous every woman in the café was gawking at him. Resolutely, she lifted her gaze to his, refusing to be one of them.

He took a sip of his espresso. Set the cup down, his gaze on her. "Your father is having trouble with the bakery?"

She frowned. "You heard that part too?"

"Sì. I had a phone call to make. I thought I'd let the

lineup die down." He cocked his head to the side. "You once said he makes the best cannoli in the Bronx. Why is business so dire?"

"The rent," she said flatly. "The neighborhood is booming. His landlord has gotten greedy. That, along with some unexpected expenses he's had, are killing him."

"What about a small business loan from the government?"

"We've explored that. They don't want to lend money to someone my father's age. It's too much of a risk."

A flash of something she couldn't read moved through his gaze. "In that case," he murmured, "I have a business proposition for you."

A business proposition?

Lazzero sat back in his chair and rested his cup on his thigh. "I am attending La Coppa Estiva in Milan next week." He lifted a brow. "You've heard of it?"

"Of course."

"Gianni Casale, the CEO of Fiammata, an Italian sportswear company I'm working on a deal with, will be there as will my ex, Carolina, who is married to Gianni. Gianni is very territorial when it comes to his wife. It's making it difficult to convince him he should do this deal with me, because the personal is getting mixed up with the business."

"*Are* you involved with his wife?" The question tumbled out of Chiara's mouth before she could stop it.

"No." He flashed her a dark look. "I am not Phil. It was over with Carolina when I ended it. It will, however, smooth things out considerably if I take a companion with me to Italy to convince Gianni I am of no threat to him."

Her tongue cleaved to the roof of her mouth. "You're suggesting I go to Italy with you and play your *girlfriend*?"

"Yes. I would, of course, compensate you accordingly."

"How?"

"With the money to help your father."

Her jaw dropped. "Why would you do that? Surely a man like you has dozens of women you could take to Italy."

He shook his head. "I don't want to take any of them. It will give them the wrong idea. What I *need* is someone who will be discreet, charming with my business associates and treat this as the business arrangement it would be. I think it could be an advantageous arrangement for us both."

An advantageous arrangement. A bitter taste filled her mouth. Her ex, Antonio, had proposed a *convenient arrangement.* Except in Antonio's case, she had been good enough to share his bed, but not blue-blooded enough to grace his arm in public.

Her stomach curled. Never would she voluntarily walk into that world again. Suffer that kind of humiliation. Be told she *didn't belong.* Not for all the money in the world.

She shook her head. "I'm not the right choice for this. Clearly I'm not after what I said earlier."

"That makes you the perfect choice," Lazzero countered. "This thing with Samara Jones has made my life a circus. I need someone I can trust who has no ulterior motives. Someone I don't have to worry about babysitting while I'm negotiating a multimillion-dollar deal. I just want to know she's going to keep up her end of the bargain."

"No." She waved a hand at him. "It's ridiculous. We don't even know each other. Not really."

"You've known me for over a year. We talk every day."

"Yes," she agreed, skepticism lacing her tone. "I ask you how business is, or 'What's the weather like out there, Lazzero?' Or, 'How about that presidential debate?' We spend five minutes chitchatting, then I make your espresso. End of conversation."

His sensual mouth twisted in a mocking smile. "So we have dinner together. I'm quite sure we can master the pertinent facts over a bottle of wine."

Her stomach muscles coiled. He was disconcerting

enough in his tailored, three-piece suit. She could only imagine what it would be like if he took the jacket off, loosened his tie and focused all that intensity on the woman involved over a bottle of wine. She knew exactly how that scenario went and it was not a mistake she was repeating.

"It would be impossible," she dismissed. "I have my shifts here. I can't afford to lose them."

"Trade them off."

"No," she said firmly. "I don't belong in that world, Lazzero. I have no *desire* to put myself in that world. I would stick out like a sore thumb. Not to mention the fact that I would never be believable as your current love interest."

"I disagree," he murmured, setting his espresso on the table and leaning forward, arms folded in front of him, eyes on hers. "You are beautiful, smart and adept at putting people at ease. With the right wardrobe and a little added... *gloss*, you would easily be the most stunning woman in the room."

Gloss? A slow curl of heat unraveled inside of her, coiling around an ancient wound that had never healed. "A diamond in the rough so to speak," she suggested, her voice pure frost.

His brow furrowed. "I didn't say that."

"But you meant it."

"You know what I mean, Chiara. I was giving you a compliment. La Coppa Estiva is a different world."

She flicked a wrist at him. "Exactly why I have no interest in this proposal of yours. In these high-stakes games you play. I thought I'd made that clear earlier."

His gaze narrowed. "What I *heard* was you on your soapbox making wild generalizations about men of a certain tax bracket."

"Hardly generalizations," she refuted. "You need someone to take to Italy with you because you've left a trail of refuse behind you, Lazzero. Because Gianni Casale doesn't trust you with his wife. I won't be part of aiding and abetting that kind of behavior."

"A trail of refuse?" His gaze chilled to a cool, hard ebony. "I think you're reading too many tabloids."

"I think not. You're exactly the sort of man I want nothing to do with."

"I'm not asking you to get involved with me," he rebutted coolly. "I'm suggesting you get over this personal bias you have against a man with a bank balance and solve your financial problems while you're at it. I have no doubt we can pull this off if you put your mind to it."

"No." She slid to the edge of the chair. "Ask someone else. I'm sure one of the other baristas would jump at the chance."

"I don't want them," he said evenly, "I want you." He threw an exorbitant figure of money at her that made her eyes widen. "It would go a long way toward helping your father."

Chiara's head buzzed. It would *pay* her father's rent for the rest of the year. Would be enough to get him back on his feet after the unexpected expenses he'd incurred having to replace some machinery at the bakery. But surely what Lazzero was proposing *was* insane? She could never pull this off and even if she could, it would put her smack in the middle of a world she wanted nothing to do with.

She got to her feet before she abandoned her common sense completely. "I need to get back to work."

Lazzero pulled a card out of his wallet, scribbled something on the back and handed it to her. "My cell number if you change your mind."

CHAPTER TWO

CHIARA'S HEAD WAS still spinning as she finished up her shift at the café and walked home on a gorgeous summer evening in Manhattan. She was too distracted, however, to take in the vibrant New York she loved, too worried about her father's financial situation to focus.

If he couldn't pay off the new equipment he'd purchased, he was going to lose the bakery—the only thing that seemed to get him up in the morning since her mother died. She couldn't conceive of that prospect happening. Which left Lazzero's shocking business proposition to consider.

She couldn't possibly do it. Would be crazy to even consider it. But how could she not?

Her head no clearer by the time she'd picked up groceries at the corner store for a quiet night in, she carried them up the three flights of stairs of the old brick walk-up she and Kat shared in Spanish Harlem, and let herself in.

They'd done their best to make the tiny, two-bedroom apartment warm and cozy despite its distinct lack of appeal, covering the dingy walls in a cherry-colored paint, adding dark refinished furniture from the antiques store around the corner, and topping it all off with colorful throws and pillows.

It wasn't much, but it was home.

Kat, who was busy getting ready for a date, joined her in the shoebox of a kitchen as Chiara stowed the groceries away. Possessing a much more robust social life than she, her roommate had plans to see a popular play with a new boyfriend she was crazy about. At the moment, however, lounging against the counter in a tomato-red silk dress and impossibly slender black heels, her roommate was hot on the trail of a juicy story.

"So," she said. "What really happened with Lazzero Di Fiore today? And no blowing me off like you did earlier."

Chiara—who thought Kat should've been a lawyer rather than the doctor she was training to be, she was so relentless in the pursuit of the facts—stowed the carton of milk in the fridge and stood up. "You can't say anything to anyone."

Kat lifted her hands. "Who am I going to tell?"

Chiara filled her in on Lazzero's business proposition. Kat's eyes went as big as saucers. "He's always had the hots for you. Maybe he's making his move."

Chiara cut that idea off at the pass. "It is strictly a business arrangement. He made that clear."

"And you said *no*? Are you crazy?" Her friend waved a red tipped hand at her. "He is offering to solve all your financial problems, Chiara, for a *week in Italy*. La Coppa Estiva is the celebrity event of the season. Most women would give their right arm to be in your position. Not to mention the fact that Lazzero Di Fiore is the hottest man on the face of the planet. What's not to like?"

Chiara pressed her lips together. Kat didn't know about her history with Antonio. Why Milan was the last place she'd want to be. It wasn't something you casually dropped into conversation with your new roommate, despite how close she and Kat had been getting.

She pursed her lips. "I have my shifts at the café. I need that job."

"Everyone's looking for extra hours right now. Someone will cover for you." Kat stuck a hand on her silk-clad hip. "When's the last time you had a holiday? Had some

fun? Your life is boring, Chiara. *Booorrring*. You're a senior citizen at age twenty-six."

A hot warmth tinged her cheeks. Her life *was* boring. It
revolved around work and more work. When she wasn't on
at the café, she was helping out at the bakery on the weekends. There was no *room* for relaxation.

The downstairs buzzer went off. Kat disappeared in a
cloud of perfume. Chiara cranked up the air-conditioning
against the deadly heat, which wouldn't seem to go below
a certain lukewarm temperature no matter how high she
turned it up, and made herself dinner.

She ate while she played with a design of a dress she'd
seen a girl wearing at the café today, but hadn't quite had
the urban chic she favored. Changing the hemline to an
angular cut and adding a touch of beading to the bodice,
she sketched it out, getting close to what she'd envisioned,
but not quite. The heat oppressive, the blaring sound of
the television from the apartment below destroying her
concentration, she threw the sketchbook and pencil aside.

What was the point? she thought, heart sinking. She
was never going to have the time or money to pursue her
career in design. Those university classes she'd taken at
Parsons had been a waste of time and money. All she was
doing was setting herself up for more disappointment in
harboring these dreams of hers, because they were never
going to happen.

Cradling her tea between her hands, she fought a bitter
wave of loneliness that settled over her, a deep, low throb
that never seemed to fade. *This* was the time she'd treasured
the most—those cups of tea after dinner with her mother
when the bakery was closed.

A seamstress by trade, her mother had been brilliant
with a needle. They'd talked while they'd sewed—about
anything and everything. About Chiara's schoolwork, about
that nasty boy in her class who was giving her trouble,

about the latest design she'd sketched at the back of her notebook that day. Until life as she'd known it had ended forever on a Friday evening when she was fifteen when her mother had sat her down to talk—not about boys or clothes—but about the breast cancer she'd been diagnosed with. By the next fall, she'd been gone. There had been no more cups of tea, no more confidences, only a big, scary world to navigate as her father had descended into his grief and anger.

The heavy, pulsing weight encompassing all of her now, she rolled to her feet and walked to the window. Hugging her arms tight around herself, she stared out at the colorful graffiti on the apartment buildings across the street. Usually, she managed to keep the hollow emptiness at bay, convince herself that she liked it better this way, because to engage was to *feel*, and to feel hurt too much. But tonight, imagining the fun, glamorous evening Kat was having, she felt scraped raw inside.

For a brief moment in time, she'd had a taste of that life. The fun and frivolity of it. She'd met Antonio at a party full of glamorous types in Chelsea last summer when a fellow barista who traveled in those circles had invited her along. The newly minted vice president of his family's prestigious global investment firm, Antonio Fabrizio had been gorgeous and worldly, intent on having her from the first moment he'd seen her.

She'd been seduced by the effortless glamour of his world, by the beguiling promises he'd made. By the command and authority he seemed to exert over everything around him. By how grounded he'd made her feel for the first time since her mother had died. Little had she known, she'd only been a diversion. That the woman Antonio was slated to marry was waiting for him at home in Milan. That she'd only been his American plaything, a "last fling" before he married.

Antonio had tried to placate her when she'd found out, assuring her his was a marriage of convenience, a fortuitous match for the Fabrizios. That *she* was the one he really wanted. In fact, he'd insisted, nothing would change. He would set her up in her own apartment and she would become his mistress.

Chiara had thrown the offer in his face, along with his penthouse key, shocked he would even think she would be interested in that kind of an arrangement. But Antonio, in his supreme arrogance, had been furious with her for walking out on him. Had pursued her relentlessly in the six months since, sending her flowers, jewelry, tickets to the opera, all of which she'd returned with a message to leave her alone, until finally he had.

Her mouth set as she stared out at the darkening night, a bitter anger sweeping through her. She had changed since him. *He* had made her change. She had become tougher, wiser to the world. *She* was not to blame for what had happened, Antonio was. Why should she be so worried about seeing him again?

If this was, as Lazzero had reasoned, a business proposition, why not turn it around to her own advantage? Use the world that had once used her? Surely she could survive a few days in Milan playing Lazzero's love interest if it meant saving her father's bakery? And if she were to run into Antonio at La Coppa Estiva, which was a real possibility, so what? It was crazy to let him have this power over her still.

She fell asleep on the sofa, the TV still on, roused by Kat at 2 a.m., who sent her stumbling to bed. When she woke for her early morning shift at the café, her decision was made.

Di Fiore's was blissfully free of its contingent of fortune hunters when Lazzero met Santo for a beer on Saturday night to talk La Coppa Estiva and their strategy for Gianni Casale.

He'd been pleasantly surprised when Chiara had called him earlier that afternoon to accept his offer. Was curious to find out why she had. Thinking he could nail those details down along with his game plan for Gianni, he'd arranged to meet her here for a drink after his beer with Santo.

Ensconcing themselves at the bar so they could keep an eye on the door, he and Santo fleshed out a multilayered plan of attack, with contingencies for whatever objections the wily Italian might present. Satisfied they had it nailed, Lazzero leaned back in his stool and took a sip of his beer. Eyed his brother's dark suit.

"Work or pleasure tonight?"

"Damion Howard and his agent are dropping by to pick up their tickets for next week. Thought I'd romance them a bit while I'm at it."

"What?" Lazzero derided. "No beautiful blonde lined up for your pleasure?"

"Too busy." Santo sighed. "This event is a monster. I need to keep my eye on the ball."

Lazzero studied the lines of fatigue etching his brother's face. "You should let Dez handle the athletes. It would free up your time."

His brother cocked a brow. "Says the ultimate control freak?"

Lazzero shrugged. He was a self-professed workaholic. Knew the demons that drove him. It was part of the territory when your father self-destructed, leaving his business and your life in pieces. No amount of success would ever convince him it was *enough*.

Santo gave him an idle look. "Did Nico tell you about his conversation with Carolina?"

Lazzero nodded. Carolina Casale, an interior designer by trade, was coordinating the closing night party for La Coppa Estiva, a job perfectly suited to her extensive project management skills. Nico, who'd negotiated a reprieve from the wedding planning to attend the party with a client, had called her to request an additional couple of tickets for some VIPs, only to find himself consoling a weepy Carolina instead, who had spent the whole conversation telling him how unhappy she was. She'd finished by asking how Lazzero was.

His fingers tightened around his glass. *He could not go through another of those scenes.* It was not his fault Carolina had married a man old enough to be her father.

"I'm working on a solution to that," he said grimly. "Tonight, in fact. Speaking of solutions, you aren't giving me too much field time are you? I can feel my knee creaking as we speak."

Santo's mouth twitched. "I'm afraid the answer is yes. We need a solid midfielder. But it's perfect, actually. Gianni plays midfield."

Lazzero was about to amplify his protest when his brother's gaze narrowed on the door. "Now *she* could persuade me to abandon my plans for the evening."

Lazzero turned around. Found himself equally absorbed by the female standing in the doorway. Her slender body encased in a sheer, flowing blouse that ended at midthigh, her dark jeans tucked into knee-high boots, Chiara had left her hair loose tonight, the silky waves falling to just below her shoulder blades in a dark, shiny cloud.

It wasn't the most provocative outfit he'd ever seen, but with Chiara's curves, she looked amazing. The wave of lust that kicked him hard in the chest irritated the hell out of him. She had labeled him a bloody Lothario, for God's sake. Had told him he was exactly the kind of man she'd never get involved with. He'd do well to remember this was a business arrangement they were embarking on together.

Chiara's scan of the room halted when she found him sitting at the bar. Santo's gaze moved from Chiara to him. "*She's* the one you're meeting?"

"My date for Italy," Lazzero confirmed, sliding off the stool.

"Who *is* she?" His brother frowned. "She looks familiar."

"Her name is Chiara. And she's far too nice a girl for you."

"Which means she's *definitely* too nice for you," Santo tossed after his retreating figure.

Lazzero couldn't disagree. Which was why he was going to keep this strictly business. Pulling to a halt in front of her, he bent to press a kiss to both of her cheeks. An intoxicating scent of orange blossom mixed with a musky, sensual undertone assailed his senses. It suited her perfectly.

"I'm sorry I'm late," she murmured, stepping back. "The barista who was supposed to relieve me was sick. I had to wait until the sub came in."

"It's fine. I was having a beer with my brother." Lazzero whisked her past Santo just as his brother's clients walked in. Chiara cocked her head to the side. "You're not going to introduce us?"

"Not now, no."

"Because I'm a barista?" A spark of fire flared in her green eyes.

"Because my brother likes to ask too many questions," he came back evenly. "Not to mention the fact that we don't have our story straight yet."

"Oh." The heat in her eyes dissipated. "That's true."

"Just for the record," he murmured, pressing a palm to the small of her back to guide her through the crowd, "Santo and I started Supersonic from nothing. We *had* nothing. There is no judgment here about what you do."

Her long dark lashes swept down, dusting her cheeks like miniature black fans. "Is it true what Samara Jones said about you and your brother masterminding your business from here?"

His mouth twisted. "It's become a bit of an urban myth, but yes, we brainstormed the idea for Supersonic at a table near the back when we were students at Columbia. We kept the table for posterity's sake when we bought the place a few years later." He arched a brow at her. "Would you like to sit there? It's nothing special," he warned.

"Yes." She surprised him by answering in the affirmative. "I'll need to know these things about you to make this believable."

"Perhaps," he suggested, his palm nearly spanning her delicate spine as he directed her around a group of people, "you'll discover other things that surprise you. Why did you say yes, by the way?"

"Because my father needs the money. I couldn't afford to say no."

Direct. To the point. Just like the woman who felt so soft and feminine beneath his hand, but undoubtedly had a spine of steel. He was certain she was up to the challenge he was about to hand her.

Seating her at the old, scarred table located in a quiet alcove off the main traffic of the bar, he pushed her chair in and sat opposite her. His long legs brushed hers as he arranged them to get comfortable. Chiara shifted away as if burned. He smothered a smile at her prickly demeanor. *That* they would have to solve if they were going to make this believable.

She traced a finger over the deep indentation carved into the thick mahogany wood, a rough impersonation of the Supersonic logo. "Who did this?"

"I did." A wry smile curved his mouth. "I nearly got us kicked out of here for good that night. But we were so high on the idea we had, we didn't care."

She sat back in her chair, a curious look on her face. "How did you make it happen, then, if you started with nothing?"

"Santo and I put ourselves through university on sports scholarships. We knew a lot of people in the industry, knew what athletes wanted in a product. Supersonic became a 'by athletes, for athletes' line." He lifted a shoulder. "A solid business plan brought our godfather on board for an initial investment, some athletes we went to school with made up the rest."

A smile played at her mouth. "And then you parlayed it into one of the world's most successful athletic-wear companies. Impressive."

"With some detours along the way," he amended. "It's a bitterly competitive industry. But we had a vision. It worked."

"Will Santo be in Milan?"

He nodded. "He's the chairman of the event. He'll have his hands full massaging all of our relationships. When he isn't busy doing that with his posse of women," he qualified drily.

"Clearly runs in the family," Chiara murmured.

Lazzero set a considering gaze on her. "I think you would be surprised by the actual number of relationships I engage in versus what the tabloids print. I do need some time to run a Fortune 500 company, after all."

"So actually," Chiara suggested, "you are a choir boy."

A smile tugged at his lips. "I wouldn't go that far."

Chiara expelled a breath as a pretty waitress arrived to take their order. In dark jeans and a navy T-shirt, Lazzero was elementally attractive in a way few men could ever hope to emulate. When he smiled, however, he was devastating. It lit up the rugged, aggressive lines of his face, highlighting his beautiful bone structure and the sensual line of his mouth. Made him beautiful in a jaw-dropping kind of way. And that was before you got to his intense black stare that seemed to dissect you into your various assorted parts.

Which was clearly having its effect on their waitress. Dressed in a gray Di Fiore's T-shirt and tight black pants, she flashed Lazzero a high-wattage smile and babbled out the nightly specials. Without asking Chiara's preference, Lazzero rattled off a request for a bottle of Italian red, spring water and an appetizer for them to share.

She eyed him as the waitress disappeared. "Are you always this...*domineering*?"

"Sì," he murmured, eyes on hers. "Most women like it when I take control. It makes them feel feminine and cared for. They don't have to think—they just sit back and... enjoy."

A wave of heat stained her cheeks, her pulse doing a wicked little jump. "I am not most women. And I *like* to think."

"I'm beginning to get that impression," he said drily. "The 'not like most women' part."

"What happens," she countered provocatively, "when you turn this hopelessly addicted contingent of yours back out into the wild? Isn't that exactly the problem you're facing with Carolina Casale?"

He shrugged. "Carolina knew the rules."

"Which are?"

"It lasts as long as she keeps it interesting."

Her jaw dropped. His arrogance was astounding. Carolina, however, had likely believed she was different—her cardinal mistake. As had been hers.

"She married Gianni on the rebound from you," she guessed.

"Perhaps."

She felt a stab of sympathy for Carolina Casale. She knew how raw those dashed hopes felt. Antonio had married within months of their breakup. Because that was what transactionally motivated men like Antonio and Lazzero did. They used people for their own purposes without thought for the consequences. It didn't matter who got hurt in the process.

The waitress returned and poured their wine. Chiara put the conversation firmly back on a business footing after she'd left. "Shall we talk details, then?"

"Yes." Lazzero sat back in his chair, glass in hand. "La Coppa Estiva is a ten-day-long event. It begins next Wednesday with the opening party, continues with the tournament, then wraps up on the following Saturday with the final game and closing party. We will need to leave New York on Tuesday night to fly overnight to Milan."

Her stomach lurched. She was actually doing this.

"That's fine," she said. "There's a girl at work who's looking for extra shifts. I can trade them off."

"Good." He inclined his head. "Have you ever been to Milan?"

She shook her head. "We have family there, but I've never been."

"The game," he elaborated, "is held at the stadium in San Siro, on the outskirts of the city. We'll be staying at my friend Filippo Giordano's luxury hotel in Milan."

Her stomach curled at the thought of sharing a hotel suite with Lazzero. But of course, they were supposedly together and they would be expected to share a room. Which got her wondering. "How do you expect us to act together? I mean—"

"How do I normally act with my girlfriends?"

"Yes."

He shrugged. "I don't expect you to be all over me. But if there is an appropriate moment where some kind of affection is in order, we go with the flow."

Which could involve a kiss. Her gaze landed on his full, sensual mouth, her stomach doing a funny roll as she imagined what it would be like to kiss him. It would be far from forgettable, she concluded with a shiver. That mouth was simply far too...*erotic*.

Which was exactly how she should *not* be thinking.

"You were right," she admitted, firmly redirecting her thoughts. "I don't have the appropriate clothes for this type of an event. I would make them, but I don't have time."

Lazzero waved a hand at her. "That comes with the deal. We have a stylist we use for our commercial shoots. Micaela's offered to outfit you on Monday."

She stiffened. "I don't need a stylist."

He shrugged. "I can send my PA with you with my credit card. But you would lose the benefit of Micaela's experience with an event like this. Which could be invaluable."

She hated the idea of his PA accompanying her even more than she hated the idea of the stylist. And, she grumpily conceded, a stylist's help would be invaluable given her doubts about her ability to pull this off.

"Fine," she capitulated, "the stylist is fine."

"*Bene.* Which brings us to the public story of *us* we will use."

She eyed him. "What were you thinking?"

"I thought we would go with the truth. That we met at the café."

"And you couldn't resist my espressos, nor me?" she filled in sardonically.

His mouth curved. "Now you're getting into the spirit. Except," he drawled, his ebony gaze resting on hers, "I would have gone with the endlessly beautiful green eyes, the razor-sharp brain and the elusive challenge of finding out who the real Chiara Ferrante is underneath all those layers."

Her heart skipped a beat. "There isn't anything to find out."

"No?" His perusal was the lazy study of a big cat. "I could have sworn there was."

"Then you'd be wrong," she came back evenly. "How long has this supposed relationship of ours been going on, then?"

"Let's say a couple of blissful months. So blissful, in fact, that I just put an engagement ring on your finger."

She gaped at him. "You never said anything about being engaged."

He hiked a broad shoulder. "If I put a ring on your finger, it will be clear to Carolina there is no hope for a reconciliation between us."

"Does she think there is?"

"Her marriage is on the rocks. She's unhappy. Gianni is worried he can't hold her."

"Oh, my God," she breathed. "Why don't you just tell Gianni he has nothing to worry about? That you have a heart of stone."

He reached into his jeans pocket and retrieved a box. Flipping it open, he revealed the ring inside. "I think *this* will be more effective. It looked like you. What do you think?"

Her jaw dropped at the enormous asscher-cut diamond with its halo of pave-set stones embedded into the band. It was the most magnificent thing she'd ever seen.

"Lazzero," she said unsteadily. "I did not sign on for this. This is *insane*."

"Think of it as a prop, that's all." He picked up her left hand and slid the glittering diamond on her index finger. Her heart thudded as she drank in how perfectly it suited her hand. How it fit like a glove. How warm and strong his fingers were wrapped around hers, tattooing her skin with the pulse of attraction that beat between them.

How *crazy* this was.

She tugged her hand free. "You can't possibly expect me to wear this. What if I put it down somewhere? What if I lose it?"

"It's insured. There's no need to worry."

"How much is it worth?"

"A couple million."

She yanked the ring off her hand. "No," she said, setting it on the table in front of him. "Absolutely not. Get something cheaper."

"I am not," he said calmly, "giving you a cheaper engagement ring because you are afraid of losing it. Carolina will be all over it. She will notice."

"And what happens when we call this off?" She searched desperately for objections. "What is Gianni going to think about that?"

"I should have him on board by then. We can let it die a slow death when we get back." He took her hand and slid the ring on again.

"I won't sleep," Chiara murmured, staring at the ring, her heart pounding. Not when she would publicly, if only for a few days, be branded the future Mrs. Lazzero Di Fiore. It *was* crazy. *She* would be crazy to agree to do this.

She should shut it down right now. *Would*, if she were wise. But as she and Lazzero sat working out the remaining details, she couldn't seem to find the words to say no. Because saving her father's business was all that mattered. Pulling him out of this depression that was breaking her heart.

CHAPTER THREE

Chiara, in fact, didn't sleep. She spent Sunday morning bleary-eyed, nursing a huge cup of coffee while she filled out the passport application Lazzero was going to fast-track for her in the morning.

The dazzling diamond on her finger flashed in the morning sunlight—a glittering, unmistakable reminder of what she'd signed on to last night. Her heart lurched in her chest, a combination of caffeine and nerves. Playing Lazzero's girlfriend was one thing. Playing his *fiancée* was another matter entirely. She was quickly developing a massive, severe case of cold feet.

She would be to Italy and back—*unengaged*—in ten days' time, she reassured herself. No need to panic or for anyone to know. Except for her father, given she wouldn't be able to help out at the bakery on the weekends. Nor could she check in on him as she always did every night, a fact that left her with an uneasy feeling in the pit of her stomach.

She chewed on her lip as she eyed her cell phone. Telling her father the truth about the trip was not an option. He would never approve of what she was doing, nor would his pride allow him to take the money. Lazzero, for whom logistics were clearly never a problem, had offered to make an angel donation to her father's business through a community organization Supersonic supported which provided assistance to local businesses.

Which solved the problem of the money. It did not, however, help with the little white lie she was going to have to tell her father about why she was going to Italy. Her father had always preached the value of keeping an impeccable truth with yourself and with others. It will, he always said, save you much heartache in life. But in this case, she concluded, the end justified the means.

She called her father and told him she was going to be vacationing with friends in a house they'd rented in Lake Como, feeling like a massive ball of guilt by the time she'd gotten off the phone. Giving in to her need to ensure he would be okay while she was gone, she called Frankie De-Lucca, an old friend of her father's who lived down the street, and asked him to look in on her father while she was away.

She dragged her feet all the way down to meet Gareth, Lazzero's driver, the next morning for her shopping expedition with Micaela Parker. She was intimidated before she'd even stepped out of the car as it halted in front of the posh Madison Avenue boutique where she was to meet the stylist. Everything in the window screamed *one month's salary*.

Micaela was waiting for her in the luxurious lounge area of the boutique. An elegant blonde, all long, lean legs, she was more interesting looking than beautiful. But she was so perfectly put together in jeans, a silk T-shirt and a blazer, funky jewelry at her wrists and neck, Chiara could only conclude she was in excellent hands. Micaela was, after all, the dresser of a quarter of Manhattan's celebrities.

"Tell me a bit about your personal style," Micaela prompted over coffee.

Chiara showed her a few of her own pieces she'd made on her phone. Micaela gave them a critical appraisal. "I like them," she said finally. "Very Coachella boho. Those soft feminine lines look great on you."

"Within reason." A pang moved through her at the praise. "I have too many curves."

"You have perfect curves. You just need to show them off properly." Micaela handed back her phone. "What other staples do you have in your wardrobe we can work with?"

Not much, it turned out.

"Not a problem," Micaela breezed. "We'll get you everything. Luckily," she teased, "Lazzero's PA gave me carte blanche. He must be seriously smitten with you."

Chiara decided no answer was better than attempting one to that statement. Micaela took the hint and reached for her coffee cup to get started. Her eyes nearly popped out of her head when she saw the giant diamond sparkling on Chiara's hand.

"You and Lazzero are *engaged*?"

"It's brand-new," Chiara murmured, as every assistant in the shop turned to stare. "We haven't made a formal announcement yet."

"You won't have to now," Micaela said drily, inclining her head toward the shop girls. "Half the city will know by noon."

Oh, God. Chiara bit her lip. Why had she agreed to do this again?

Micaela led her into the dressing area and started throwing clothes at her with military-like precision. Telling herself it was the armor she needed to face a world in which she'd been declared not good enough, Chiara tried on everything the stylist presented her with and discovered Micaela had impeccable taste that worked well with her own personal style.

It was when they came to the search for the perfect evening dresses that Micaela got intensely critical. Chiara would be in the limelight on these occasions, photographed by paparazzi from around the world. They needed to be flawless. Irreproachable. Eye-catching, but not ostentatious.

Just the thought of walking down a red carpet made her stomach churn.

By the time they'd chosen purses and jewelry to go with her new wardrobe, she was ready to drop. Looking forward to collapsing at the spa appointment Micaela had booked for her, she protested when the stylist dragged her next door to the lingerie boutique.

"I don't need any of that," she said definitively. "I'm good."

"Are you sure what you have isn't going to leave lines?" Micaela asked.

No dammit, she wasn't. And she wasn't about to end up on a red carpet with them. Marching into the fitting room, she tried on the beautiful lingerie Micaela handed over. Felt her throat grow tighter as she stood in front of the mirror in peach silk, the lace on the delicate bra the lingerie's only nod to fuss.

Antonio had loved to buy her lingerie. Had always said it was because he loved having her all to himself—that he didn't want to share her with anyone else. He'd used that excuse when it came to social engagements too—taking her to low-key restaurants rather than his high-profile events because, she'd assumed, he was deciding whether he should make her a Fabrizio or not, and fool that she'd been, she hadn't wanted to mess it up.

Heat lashed her cheeks. Never again would she give a man that power over her. Never again would she be so deluded about the truth.

Sinking her fingers into the clasp of the delicate bra, she stripped it off. She hadn't quite shed the sting of the memory when Micaela whisked her off to the salon for lunch, hair and treatments.

Dimitri, whom Micaela proclaimed the best hair guy in Manhattan, promptly suggested she cut her hair to shoulder length and add bangs for a more sophisticated look.

A rejection rose in her throat, an automatic response, because her hair had always been her thing. Her kryptonite. Antonio had loved it.

That lifted her chin. She wasn't that Chiara anymore. She wanted all signs of her gone. And if there was a chance she was going to run into Antonio in Milan, she would need *all* her armor in place.

"Cut it off," she said to Dimitri. "And yes to the bangs."

Lazzero was on the phone tying up a loose end before he left for Europe on Tuesday evening when Chiara walked into the tiny lounge at Teterboro Airport. Gareth, who'd dropped her off with Lazzero's afternoon meetings on the other side of town, deposited Chiara's suitcase beside her, gave him a wave and melted back outside. But Lazzero was too busy looking at Chiara to notice.

Dressed in black cigarette pants, another pair of those sexy boots she seemed to favor and a silk shirt that skimmed the curve of her amazing backside, she looked cool and sophisticated. It was her hair that had him aghast. Gone were the thick, silky waves that fell down her back, in their place a blunt bob that just skimmed her shoulders. He couldn't deny the sophisticated style and wispy bangs accentuated her lush features and incredible eyes. It just wasn't *her*.

Wrapping up the call, he strode across the lounge toward her. "What the hell did you do to your hair?"

Her eyes widened, a flash of defiance firing their green depths. "It was time for a change. Dimitri, Micaela's hair guy, thinks it looks sophisticated. Wasn't that what you were going for?"

Yes. *No.* Not if it meant cutting her hair. She had gorgeous hair. *Had* gorgeous hair. He wanted to inform *Dimitri* he was an idiot. Except Chiara looked exactly like the type of woman he'd have on his arm. Micaela had done her job well. *So why the hell was he so angry?* Because he'd liked her better the way she'd been before?

"I'm sorry," he said gruffly. "It's been a long day. You look beautiful. And yes, it's chic…very sophisticated."

Her chin lowered a fraction. "Micaela was amazing. She gave me some excellent advice."

"Good." Catching a signal from a waiting official, he inclined his head. "We're good to go. You ready?"

She nodded and went to pick up her bag. He bent to take it from her, his fingers brushing against hers as he did. She flinched and took a step back. He grimaced and hoisted the bag. He was going to have to deal with that reaction before they landed in Italy or this relationship between them wasn't going to be remotely believable.

He carried it and his own bag onto the tarmac, where the sleek corporate jet was waiting. After a quick check of their passports, they were airborne, winging their way across the Atlantic.

He pulled out his laptop as soon as they'd leveled out. Chiara, an herbal tea in hand, fished out a magazine and started reading.

Together they silently coexisted, seated across from each other in the lounge area. Appreciating the time to catch up and finding it heartily refreshing to be with a woman who didn't want to chatter all the way across the ocean about inane things he wasn't the slightest bit interested in, it wasn't until a couple of hours later that he noticed Chiara wasn't really focusing on anything. Staring out the window in between flipping pages, applying multiple coats of lip balm and fidgeting to the point where he finally sighed and set his laptop aside.

"Okay," he murmured. "What's wrong?"

She dug into her bag, pulled out a newspaper and dropped it on the table in front of him. Too busy to have touched the inch-thick pile of press clippings that had been left on his desk that morning, he picked it up and scanned the tabloid page, finding the story Chiara was referring to near the bottom. It was Samara Jones's weekly column, featuring a shot of Chiara leaving a store, shopping bags in hand.

One Down—One to Go!

Sorry, ladies, but this Di Fiore is now taken. According to my sources, Lazzero Di Fiore's new fiancée was seen shopping in fashion hot spot Zazabara on Monday with celebrity stylist Micaela Parker, a four-carat asscher-cut diamond dazzling on her finger. My source wouldn't name names, but revealed an appearance at La Coppa Estiva was the impetus for the shopping excursion.

Lazzero threw the tabloid down. For once he didn't feel like strangling the woman. It was perfect, actually. Word would get around, Carolina would realize the reality of the situation and his problem would be solved.

The pinched expression on Chiara's face, however, made it clear she didn't feel the same way. "It was the point of this, after all," he reasoned. "Don't sweat it. It will be over in a few days."

She shot him a deadly look. "Don't sweat it? Playing your girlfriend is one thing, Lazzero. Having my face plastered across one of New York's dailies as your fiancée is another matter entirely. What if my father sees it? Not to mention the fact that it's going to be the shortest engagement in history. The press will have a field day with it."

He shrugged. "You knew they were going to photograph you in Milan."

"I was hoping it would get buried on page twenty." Her

mouth pursed. "Honestly, I have no idea how we're going to pull this off."

"We won't," he said meaningfully, "if you flinch every time I touch you."

A rosy pink dusted her cheeks. "I don't do that."

"Yes, you do." *Now*, he decided, was the time to get to the bottom of the enigmatic Chiara Ferrante.

"Have a drink with me before dinner."

She frowned. "I'm sure you have far too much work to do."

"It's an eight-hour flight. There's plenty of time. You just said it yourself," he pointed out. "We need to work on making this relationship believable if we're going to pull this off. Part of that is getting to know each other better."

Summoning the attendant, he requested a predinner drink, stood and held out a hand to her.

Chiara took the hand Lazzero offered and rolled to her feet. She could hardly say no. He would only accuse her of being prickly again. And she thought that maybe he was right, maybe if they got to know each other better she wouldn't feel so apprehensive about what she was walking into. About her ability to carry this charade off.

She curled up beside him on the sofa in the lounge area, shoes off, legs tucked beneath her. Tried to relax as she took a sip of her drink, but it was almost impossible to do so with Lazzero looking so ridiculously attractive in dark pants and a white shirt rolled up at the sleeves, dark stubble shadowing his jaw. It was just as disconcerting as she'd imagined it would be. As if the testosterone level had been dialed up to maximum in the tiny airplane cabin with nowhere to go.

God. She took another sip of her drink. Grasped on to the first subject that came to mind. "What sport did you play in university?"

"Basketball." He sat back against the sofa and crossed one long leg over the other. "It was my obsession."

"Santo too?"

His mouth curved. "Santo is too pretty to rough it up. He'd be running straight to his plastic surgeon if he ever got an elbow to the face. Santo played baseball."

She considered him curiously. "How good *were* you? You must have been talented to put yourself through school on a full scholarship."

He shrugged. "I was good. But an injury in my senior year put me on the sidelines. I didn't have enough time to get back to the level I needed to be before the championships and draft." He pursed his lips. "It wasn't meant to be."

She absorbed his matter-of-fact demeanor. She didn't think it could have been so simple. Giving up her design classes had been like leaving a piece of herself behind when money had been prioritized for the bakery. Lazzero had had his fingers on every little boy's dream of becoming a professional athlete, only to have it slip right through them.

"That must have been difficult," she observed, "to have your dream stolen from you."

A cryptic look moved across his face. "Some dreams are too expensive to keep."

"Supersonic was a dream you and your brothers had," she pointed out.

"Which was built on a solid business case backed up by a gap in the market we identified. Opportunity," he qualified, "makes sense to me. Blind idealism does not."

"Too much ambition can also be destructive," she said. "I see plenty of examples of that in New York."

"In the man who broke your heart?" Lazzero inserted smoothly.

Her pulse skipped a beat. "Who says he exists?"

"I do," he drawled. "Your speech at the café...the fact that you've never given any man who comes in there a fighting chance. You have 'smashed to smithereens' written all over you."

She sank her teeth into her lip, finding that an all-too-accurate description of what Antonio had done to her. "There was someone," she acknowledged quietly, "and yes, he broke my heart. But in hindsight, it was for the best. It made me see his true colors."

"Which were?"

"That he was not to be trusted. That men like him are not to be trusted."

He eyed her. "That is a massive generalization. So he hurt you...so he burned you badly. He is only *one* man, Chiara. What are you going to do? Spend the rest of your life avoiding a certain kind of man because he *might* hurt you?"

Her mouth set at a stubborn angle. "I'm not willing to take the risk."

"Did you love him?"

"I thought I did." She gave him a pointed look. "I could ask you the same thing. Where does *your* fear of commitment come from? Because clearly, you have one."

A lift of his broad shoulder. "I simply don't care to."

"Why not?"

"Because relationships are complicated dramas I have no interest in participating in." He took a sip of his drink. Rested his glass on his lean, corded thigh. "What about family?" he asked, tipping his glass at her. "I know nothing about yours other than the fact that your father, Carlo, runs Ferrante's. What about your mother? Brothers? Sisters?"

A shadow whispered across her heart. "My mother died of breast cancer when I was fifteen. I'm an only child."

His gaze darkened. "I'm sorry. You were close to her?"

"Yes," she said quietly. "She ran the bakery with my father. She was amazing—wonderful, *wise*. A pseudo parent to half the kids in the neighborhood. My father always said most of the clientele came in just to talk to her."

"You miss her," he said.

Heat stung the back of her eyes. "Every day." It was a deep, dark hollow in her soul that would never be filled.

Lazzero curled his fingers around hers. Strong and protective, they imparted a warmth that seemed to radiate right through her. "My father died when I was nineteen," he murmured. "I know how it feels."

Oh. She bit her lip. "How?"

"He was an alcoholic. He drank himself to death."

She absorbed his matter-of-fact countenance. "And your mother? Is she still alive?"

He nodded. "She's remarried and lives in California."

"Do you see her much?"

He shook his head. "She isn't a part of our lives."

"Why not?"

"It isn't relevant to this discussion."

She sat back in the sofa as a distinct chill filled the air. *Not a part of their lives?* What did that mean? From the closed-off look on Lazzero's face, it didn't seem as if she was going to find out.

She slid her hand out of his. Took a sip of her drink. "What other things should I know about you?" she asked, deciding the mood needed lightening. "Recreational pursuits? Likes, dislikes?"

His mouth quirked. "Are you looking for the dating show answer?"

"If you like," she agreed.

He took a sip of his wine. Cradled the glass in his palm. "I train in a gym every morning at six with a fighter from the old neighborhood. That's about the extent of my recreational activities other than the odd pickup basketball game with my brothers. I *appreciate*," he continued, eyes glimmering with humor, "honesty and integrity in a person as well as fine Tuscan wines. I *dislike* Samara Jones."

Her mouth curved as she considered her response.

"You've likely gathered from my speech at the café integrity is a big one for me too," she said, picking up on the theme. "*I*, like you, have little downtime. When I'm not working at the café, I'm helping out at the bakery, which makes my life utterly mundane. Although I do," she admitted with a self-deprecating smile, "have a secret obsession with ballroom dancing reality shows. It's the escapism."

Lazzero arched a brow. "Do you? Dance?"

"No." She made a face. "I'm horrible. It's entirely aspirational. You?"

"My mother was a dancer, so yes. She made us take classes. She thought it was an invaluable social skill."

She found the idea of the three powerful Di Fiore brothers taking dance classes highly entertaining. It occurred to her then that she had no idea what a date with Lazzero would look like. Did he take a woman dancing? Perhaps he whisked them off to Paris for lavish dinner dates? Or were the females in his life simply plus-one accompaniments to his endless social calendar?

Was he romantic or entirely transactional? She sank her teeth into her lip. *That* had nothing to do with a business arrangement, but God, was she curious. If she and Lazzero had ever acted on the attraction between them, how would it have played out?

She decided it was a reasonable question to ask, given their situation. "So what would a typical date night look like for you? So I have some sense of what *we* would look like."

He rubbed a palm over the stubble on his jaw, a contemplative look on his face. "We might," he began thoughtfully, "start off with dinner at my favorite little Italian place in the East Village. Nothing fancy, just great food and a good atmosphere. Things would definitely be getting interesting over dinner because I consider stimulating conversation and excellent food the best primer."

For what? she wondered, her stomach coiling.

"So then," he continued, apparently electing to illuminate her, "if my date decided she'd found it as stimulating as I, we'd likely head back to my place on Fifth. You could assume she'd end up well satisfied...*somewhere* in my penthouse."

Heat flared down low, a wave of color staining her cheeks. She wasn't sure if it was the "somewhere" that got her or the "well satisfied" part.

"I see," she said evenly. "Thank you for that very *visual* impression."

"And you?" he prompted smoothly. "What are your dating preferences? Assuming, of course, they involve the working-class, non-power-hungry variety of man?"

"I'm too busy to date."

He gave her a speculative look. "When *was* the last time you had a date?"

She eyed him. "You don't need to know that. It has nothing to do with our deal."

"You're right," he deadpanned. "I just want to know."

"No," she said firmly. "It's *not relevant* to this discussion."

An amused smile tilted his lips. "You could be out of practice, you realize?"

"Out of practice for what?"

"Kissing," he said huskily, his smoky gaze dropping to her mouth. "Maybe we should try one now and get it out of the way. See if we're any good at it."

Something swooped and then dropped in her stomach. She was seriously afraid she *was* out of practice. *Severely* out of practice. But that didn't mean kissing Lazzero was a good idea. In fact, she was sure it was a very *bad* idea.

"I don't think so," she managed, past a sandpaper dry throat.

"Why not?" His ebony eyes gleamed with challenge. "Or are you afraid of the very *real* attraction between us?"

Her pulse racing a mile a minute at the thought of that sensual, erotic mouth taking hers, she could hardly deny it. She *could*, however, shut it down. *Right now.*

She lifted her chin, eyes on his. "This is a business arrangement between us, Lazzero. When we kiss, it will be toward that purpose and that purpose only. Are we clear on that?"

"Crystal," he murmured. "I like a woman who can keep her eye on the ball."

CHAPTER FOUR

CHIARA'S MIND WAS on anything but business after that heated encounter with Lazzero. By putting the attraction between them squarely out in the open, he had created a sexual awareness of each other she couldn't seem to shake. Which absolutely needed to happen because that attraction had no place in this business arrangement of theirs. Particularly when Lazzero had clearly been toying with her with his own ends in mind—making them *believable* for Gianni Casale.

She retreated to a book after dinner, forcing herself to focus on it rather than her ill-advised chemistry with the man sitting across from her. Night fell like a cloak outside the window. With Lazzero still absorbed in his seemingly endless mountain of work, her eyelids began to drift shut. Giving in to the compulsion, she accepted his invitation to use the luxurious bedroom at the back of the plane and caught a few hours of sleep.

When she woke, a golden, early morning light blanketed the white-capped Italian Alps in a magnificent, otherworldly glow. She freshened up in the bathroom, then joined Lazzero in the main cabin. He'd changed and looked crisp and ready to go in a light blue shirt and jeans, his dark stubble traded for a clean-shaven jaw.

Her heart jumped in her chest at how utterly gorgeous he was. Did the man ever look disheveled?

"We're about to land," he said, looking up from the report he was reading. "Do you want coffee and breakfast before we do?"

She wasn't the slightest bit hungry, still groggy from sleep. But she thought the sustenance might do her good. Accepting the offer, she inhaled a cup of strong, black coffee and nibbled on a croissant. Soon, they were landing in Milan and being whisked from the airport to the luxury hotel Lazzero's Milanese friend, hotel magnate Filippo Giordano, owned near the La Scala opera house.

The Orientale occupied four elegant fifteenth-century buildings that had been transformed from a spectacularly beautiful old convent into a luxurious, urban oasis. Chiara was picking her jaw up off the ground when the hotel manager swooped in to greet them.

"We were fully booked when Filippo made the request," he informed them smoothly. "La Coppa Estiva is always *maniaco*. Luckily, the presidential suite became available. Filippo thought it was perfect, given you are newly engaged."

Chiara's stomach dropped. *This is well and truly on. Oh, my God.*

The stately suite they'd been allocated occupied the entire third floor of the hotel, living up to its presidential suite status with its high ceilings and incredible views of the city, including one from the stepped-down infinity pool on the elegantly landscaped terrace.

Sunlight flooded its expansive interiors as the butler gave them a personal tour. The suite's lush, tasteful color scheme in cream and taupe was complemented by its black oak woodwork, the perfect combination of Milanese style with a touch of the Orient.

Chiara's eyes nearly bugged out of her head when the butler showed them the showpiece of a bathroom, its muted lighting, Brazilian marble floors and stand-alone hot tub occupying a space as large as her entire apartment. But it was the gorgeous, palatial bedroom with its French doors and incredible vistas that made her heart drop into her stomach. *One elegant, king-size, four-poster bed.* How was that going to work?

Lazzero eyed her. "I'd asked for a suite, thinking we'd get one with multiple rooms, but clearly this was all that was available. I'll sleep on the sofa in the bedroom."

"No." She shook her head. "You're far too tall for that. I will."

"I'm not a big sleeper." He shut the argument down with a shake of his head.

They got settled into the suite, Chiara waving off the butler who offered to hang up their things because she preferred to do it herself. After a sumptuous lunch on the terrace, Lazzero went off to work in the office, with a directive she should take a nap before the party because it was going to be a late night.

She didn't have the energy to protest yet another of his arrogant commands. Too weary from only a few hours of sleep, she undressed in the serene, beautiful bedroom and put on jersey sweats before she crawled beneath the soft-as-silk sheets of the four-poster bed. The next thing she knew, it was 6 p.m., the alarm she'd set to ensure she'd have enough time to get ready sounding in her ear.

Padding out to the living room, she discovered Lazzero was outside swimming laps in the infinity pool. Deciding she would enjoy the pool with its jaw-dropping view tomorrow, *minus* what she was sure would be an equally spectacular half-naked Lazzero, she had a late tea, then took a long, hot bath in the sunken tub.

Lazzero came in to shower as she sat applying a light coat of makeup in the dressing room. Keeping her brain firmly focused on the mascara wand in her hand rather than on the naked man in the shower, she stroked it over her lashes, transforming them from their ordinary dark abundance to a silky, lush length that swept her cheeks. A light coat of pink gloss finished the subtle look off.

Makeup and hair complete, she slipped on the silver sequined dress she and Micaela had chosen for the party. Long-sleeved and made of a gauzy, figure-hugging material, it clung to every inch of her body, the sexy open back revealing a triangle of bare, creamy flesh.

She stared dubiously at her reflection in the mirror. It was on trend, perfect for the opening party, but it was shorter than anything she normally wore. Micaela, however, had insisted she had an amazing figure and needed to show it off. She just wasn't sure she needed to show so *much* of it off.

Pushing her doubts aside, she slipped on her gold heels, a favorite purchase from her shopping trip because they were just too gorgeous to fault, and a sparkly pair of big hoop earrings, her one concession to her bohemian style. And declared herself done.

She stepped out onto the terrace to wait for Lazzero. The sun was setting on Milan, the magnificent Duomo di Milano, the stunning cathedral that sat in the heart of the city, bathed in a rosy pink light, its Gothic spires crawling high into the sky. But her mind wasn't on the spectacular scenery, it was on the night ahead.

Her stomach knotted with nerves, her fingers closing tight around the metal railing. This wasn't her world. What if she said or did something that would embarrass Lazzero? What if she stumbled on one of the answers they'd prepared to the inevitable questions about them?

Her mouth firmed. She'd been taking care of herself since she was fifteen. She'd learned how to survive in any situation life had thrown at her in tough, gritty Manhattan which would eat you alive if you let it. Every *day* at the Daily Grind was an exercise in diplomacy and small talk.

Surely she could survive a few hours socializing with the world's elite?

And perhaps, she conceded, butterflies circling her stomach, she was winding herself up for nothing over Antonio. Perhaps he wouldn't even be there tonight. Perhaps he was out of town on business. He ran a portfolio of global investments—he very likely could be.

Better to focus on the things she could control. Another of her father's favorite tenets.

Fifty laps of the infinity pool with its incomparable view of Milan should have rid Lazzero of his excess adrenaline. Or so he thought until he walked out onto the balcony and found Chiara sparkling like the brightest jewel in the night.

Dark hair shining in a silken cap that framed her beautiful face, the silver dress highlighting her hourglass figure, her insanely good legs encased in mile-high stilettos—she made his heart stutter in his chest. And that was before he got to her gorgeous eyes, lagoon-green in the fading light, a beauty mark just above one dark-winged brow lending her a distinctly exotic look.

The tension he read there snapped his brain back into working order. "Nervous?" he asked, moving to her side.

"A bit."

"Don't be," he murmured. "You look breathtakingly beautiful. I'm even forgiving Dimitri for the hair."

She tipped her head back to look up at him, her silky hair sliding against her shoulder. A charge vibrated the air between them, sizzling the blood in his veins. "You don't have to feed me lines," she murmured. "We aren't *on* yet."

His mouth curved at her prickly demeanor. "That wasn't a line. You'll soon know me well enough to know I don't deliver them, Chiara. I'm all for the truth in its soul-baring, hard-to-take true colors. Even when it hurts. So how about we make a deal? Nothing but honesty between us this week? It will make this a hell of a lot easier."

An emotion he couldn't read flickered in her eyes. She crossed her arms over her chest and leaned back against the railing. "Tell me why this deal with Gianni is so important for you, then? Why go to such lengths to secure it?"

He lifted a shoulder. "It's crucial to my company's growth plans."

She frowned. "Why so crucial? Fiammata is a fading brand, Supersonic the rising star."

"Fiammata has a shoe technology we're interested in."

"So you want to license it to use in your own designs?"

His mouth curved. "Sharp brain," he drawled. "It's one of the things I appreciate about you." Her legs being the other predominant one at the moment.

She frowned. "What's the holdup, then?"

And wasn't that the multimillion-dollar question? A thorn unearthed itself in his side, burrowing deep. "Fiammata is a family company. Gianni may be having a hard time letting such an important piece of it go."

"As would you," she pointed out, "if it was yours."

"Yes," he agreed, a wry smile twisting his mouth, "I would." He reached across her to point to the Duomo, glittering in the fading light. "There is a myth that Gian Galeazzo Visconti, the aristocrat who ordered the construction of the cathedral, was visited by the devil in his dreams. He ordered Visconti to create a church full of diabolical images or he would steal his soul. Thus the monstrous heads you see on the cathedral's facade."

"Not really much of a choice was it?" Chiara said as she turned her head to look at the magnificent cathedral.

"Not unless you intend to embrace your dark side, no." His gaze slid over the graceful curve of her neck. Noted she'd missed a hook at the back of her dress. *Perhaps more nervous than she admitted.*

He stepped behind her. "You aren't quite done up," he murmured, setting his fingers to the tiny hook. It took a moment to work out the intricate, almost invisible closure, his fingers brushing against the velvet-soft skin that covered her spine.

She went utterly still beneath his hands, the voltage that stretched between them so potent he could almost taste it. Her floral perfume drifting into his nostrils, her soft, sensual body brushing against his, the urge to act on the elemental attraction between them was almost impossible to resist. To set his hands to those delectable hips, to put his mouth to the soft, sensitive skin behind her ear until she melted back into him and offered him her mouth.

But, he admitted, past his accelerating pulse, that would be starting something he couldn't finish because the *only* thing on the agenda tonight was nailing Gianni Casale down, once and for all.

He reluctantly pulled back. Chiara exhaled an audible breath. Turned to look up at him with darkened eyes, her pupils dilated a deep black among a sea of green. "He'll be there tonight? Gianni?" she asked huskily.

"*Sì.* Everyone in Milan will be there." He glanced at his watch. "Speaking of which, we should go or we'll be late."

The sleek Lamborghini Lazzero had borrowed from Filippo made quick work of the drive to the venue. Soon, they were pulling up in front of Il Cattedrale, the historic church where the opening party for La Coppa Estiva was being held.

Turned into a café/nightclub over a decade ago, its stately facade was lit for the festivities, illuminating the cathedral's elegant red brickwork and massive arched front door. Chiara's stomach turned to stone as she took in the scores of paparazzi jostling for position on either side of the stationed-off red carpet, camera flashes snapping like mad as they photographed the arrival of the world's glitterati.

There was the world's most famous Portuguese footballer making his way down the red carpet with his supermodel girlfriend, followed by the eldest princess of a tiny European municipality Chiara recognized from one of the gossip magazines her fellow barista Lucy kept under the counter. The princess's balding, older husband beside her was, Chiara recalled, a huge fan of football.

"Santo will be excited about that," Lazzero murmured as he helped her from the car. "Free publicity right there."

Her damp palm in his, her other clutching the tiny purse that matched her dress, Chiara didn't respond. *What had Micaela said about the etiquette for the red carpet?* Her mind felt as blank as a chalkboard wiped clean.

Lazzero passed the car keys to the valet and bent his head to hers. "Relax," he said softly, his lips brushing her ear. "I will be by your side the entire time."

A current zigzagged through her, one she felt all the way to the pit of her stomach. It didn't get any better as Lazzero straightened and pressed a hand to the small of her back. In a sophisticated black tux that molded his long, muscular frame to perfection, he was undeniably elegant. *Hot.* Utterly in command of his surroundings.

She took a deep breath and nodded. The handler gave them the signal to walk. Lazzero propelled her forward, stopping in front of the logo-emblazoned step-and-repeat banner so the photographers could get a shot of them. The heat from his splayed palm radiated through her bare skin, focusing every available brain cell on those few inches of flesh.

It did the trick in distracting her. Before she could blink, it was over and they were making their way inside the cathedral. Which was *unbelievable*.

Much of the original architecture of the church had been

left intact, stone walls and square pillars made of cream-colored Italian marble rising up to greet the original sweeping balconies of the cathedral. The massive chandelier was incredible, a full story tall, the large canvases on the walls impressive. But the most arresting sight of all had to be the original altar which had been converted into a bar under the dome of the church. Lit tonight in Supersonic red, it was spectacular.

"I've never seen anything like it," Chiara breathed. "It's like we've all come to pray to the gods of entertainment."

Lazzero's mouth twisted. "Exactly what Santo was envisioning. He'll be thrilled."

The crowds were so thick they were difficult to negotiate as they made their way toward the bar, the upbeat music drowned out by the buzz of the hundreds in attendance. Lazzero wrapped a hand around her wrist, guiding her through it as they sought out his brothers who held court at the bar.

Santo, whom she remembered from Di Fiore's, looked supremely sophisticated in a dark suit with a lavender shirt, every bit the blond Adonis the press painted him as. Nico had Lazzero's dark looks, so handsome in a clean-edged, perfect kind of way, he was intimidatingly so.

Both were undeniably charming. "Trust Lazzero to show up with the most beautiful woman in the room when he claims he has been out of circulation," Nico drawled, kissing both of Chiara's cheeks. "Although you picked the wrong brother," Santo interjected, stepping forward and lifting her hand to his mouth. "Why go for the middle brother when you can have the most physically viable of them all? Think of the genetics."

He said it so straight-faced, Chiara burst out laughing. "Yes," she said, "but Lazzero tells me you have a *posse*. I'm afraid that wouldn't do for me."

Santo pouted. "I will give it up when the time comes."

"That will be when you are old and gray." Nico handed her a glass of champagne and Lazzero a tumbler of some dark-colored liquor. Lounging back against the bar, the eldest Di Fiore nodded toward a table beside the dance floor. "Gianni arrived a few minutes ago."

Chiara's gaze moved to Gianni Casale, whose powerful presence stood out amongst the crowd at the table. In his midfifties, he had thick, coarse black hair tinged with gray, expressive dark eyes and a lined face full of character. Impeccably dressed in a charcoal gray suit with a silver-gray tie, he was, she conceded, undeniably handsome still.

Her attention shifted to the woman beside him. She didn't have to wonder if it was Carolina Casale or not because the brunette's eyes were trained on her and the hand Lazzero had rested on her waist. Remarkably beautiful with vivid blue eyes that matched her designer silk dress, dark hair and alabaster skin, the cool elegance she projected was borderline aloof.

She looked, Chiara concluded, as if she'd rather be anywhere than where she was. *Hungry* was the only word she could think of to describe how Carolina looked at Lazzero. She wondered if the other woman had any idea how obvious her feelings were.

Lazzero, on the other hand, looked utterly impassive as he turned around and got the lay of the land from his brothers. When they were suitably caught up, he tightened his fingers at her waist. "We should circulate," he murmured. "You okay with the champagne?"

She pulled in a deep breath. "Yes."

Lazzero spent the next couple of hours attempting to cover off the most important business contacts in the room as he played it cool with Gianni, waiting for the Casales to come to them. He should have been focused solely on business, his game plan with Gianni firmly positioned in his head, but his attention kept straying to the woman at his side.

He was having trouble keeping his eyes off Chiara's legs in that dress, as were half the men in the room. Despite the tension he could sense in her, a tension he couldn't wholly understand given the confidence he was used to from her, she remained poised at his side, charming his business associates with that natural wit and intelligence he had always appreciated about her. It was, he found, a wholly alluring combination.

He was about to acquire another glass of champagne for her from a waiter's tray when Carolina and Gianni approached, Carolina's hand on her husband's arm firmly guiding him toward them.

His ex-lover looked stunning, as beautiful as ever with those icy cool, perfect features, but tonight she left him cold. She had always been too self-contained, too calculating, too bent on getting her own way. Gianni, who'd spent three years putting up with those character flaws, eyed him warily as they approached, his dark eyes betraying none of the undercurrents stretching between them.

"Lazzero." Dropping her hand from her husband's arm, Carolina stood on tiptoe and pressed a kiss to both of Lazzero's cheeks. She lingered a bit too long, and as she did Gianni's eyes flashed with a rare show of emotion.

"Carolina." Lazzero set her firmly away from him so that he could shake Gianni's hand. Releasing it, he drew Chiara forward. "I would like you both to meet my fiancée, Chiara Ferrante."

The color drained from Carolina's face. "I'd heard the gossip," she murmured, her gaze dropping to Chiara's left hand, where the asscher-cut diamond blazed bright. "I thought it must be wrong." She forced a tight smile to her lips as she returned her perusal to Lazzero. "You swore you'd never marry."

"Things change when you meet the right person," Lazzero said blithely.

"Apparently so."

Gianni, ever the gentleman, stepped forward to compensate for his wife's lack of discretion. *"Felicitazoni,"* he said, pressing a kiss to Chiara's cheeks. "Lazzero is a lucky man, clearly."

"Grazie mille," Chiara replied. "It's all very new. We're still...absorbing it."

"When is the big day?" Carolina lifted a brow. "I haven't seen an announcement."

"We're still working that out," said Chiara. "For now, we're just enjoying being engaged."

"I'm sure you are." A wounded look flashed through Carolina's vibrant blue eyes. "You must be very happy."

Lazzero felt a bite of guilt sink into him. He shouldn't have let it go on so long. It was a mistake he would never repeat.

Chiara escaped to the ladies' room after that awkward encounter with the Casales. She felt sorry for Carolina who was so clearly still in love with Lazzero, who hadn't blinked the entire conversation. Because she knew that hurt—that rejection—what it felt like to be discarded for something *better.*

It took her forever to wind her way through the crowd to the powder room. An oasis in the midst of the celebration, it was done in cream and black marble with muted lighting and white lilies covering every available surface. Heading for one of the leather seats in front of the mirror, Chiara ran smack into an older woman on her way out.

An apology rose to her lips. It died in her mouth as she stared at the lined, still handsome face of Esta Fabrizio, Antonio's mother. She froze, unsure of what to do. The older woman swept her gaze over her in a cursory look, not a hint of recognition flaring in her dark eyes. Flashing Chiara an apologetic look, she murmured, *"Scusi,"* then moved around her to the door.

"Is it just you and Maurizio here tonight?" Esta's companion asked.

"Sì," Esta replied. "My son is out of town, so it is us representing the family tonight."

Chiara sank down on the leather seat, relief flooding through her as they left. *Antonio isn't here.* She could put that fear to rest. But quick on its heels came humiliation as she stared at her pale face in the mirror. Esta had looked at her as if she was nothing. But why *would* she remember her?

She'd treated Chiara as if she were a bug to be crushed under her shoe the day she'd shown up unexpectedly at Antonio's penthouse to surprise him for his birthday, only to find Chiara leaving for work. Esta had taken one look at Chiara, absorbed her working-class, Bronx accent and correctly assessed the situation. She'd informed Chiara that Antonio had a fiancée in Milan. That she was simply his American "plaything." The Fabrizio matriarch had added, with a brutal lack of finesse, that a Fabrizio would never marry someone like her. So best if she ended it now.

A bitter taste filled her mouth as she reached for her purse and fumbled inside for her powder and lipstick. Applying a coat of pink gloss and powdering her nose with shaking hands, she willed herself composure. She would *not* let that woman get to her again. The important thing was that Antonio was not here. She could relax.

Now all she had to do was pull herself together.

The party was in full swing when she exited the powder room. The lights had been lowered, the massive chandelier cast a purple hue across the room, the hundreds of smaller disco balls surrounding it glittered like luminescent planets in the sky. High in the ceiling, amidst that stunning celestial display, hung sexily dressed acrobats in beautiful red dresses, hypnotizing to the eye.

Music pulsed through the room, champagne flowed freely as couples packed the dance floor. She headed toward the bar where Lazzero and Santo had ensconced themselves. Almost groaned out loud when Carolina Casale flagged her down, two glasses of champagne in her hand. *That was all she needed right now.*

Carolina handed her a glass of champagne. "I apologize for my behavior earlier. I was caught off guard. I thought I should congratulate you properly. Lazzero and I go a long way back."

"He mentioned." Chiara considered Carolina warily as she took the glass. "*Grazie.* How *do* you know each other?"

"My firm did the interior decorating for Supersonic's offices as well as Lazzero's penthouse when he bought it." A low purr vibrated Carolina's voice. "Lazzero couldn't be bothered with that kind of thing."

Heat seared her skin. She could only imagine how that relationship had started. Carolina walking around Lazzero's penthouse with paint samples in her hand only to find herself in his bed. *Well satisfied*, no doubt.

"How did *you* and Lazzero meet?" Carolina prompted, a speculative glitter in her eyes. "Everyone is very curious about how you did the impossible by catching him."

"We met in a café."

The brunette arched a dark brow. "A café?"

"Where I work." Chiara lifted her chin. "We've known each other for over a year now."

An astonished look crossed the other woman's face. "You're a *waitress*?"

"A barista," Chiara corrected, her encounter with Esta Fabrizio adding a bite to her tone. "Love doesn't discriminate, I guess."

Carolina's face fell at the surgical strike. "Love?" Her

mouth twisted. "I would offer you a piece of advice about Lazzero. He is in *lust* with you, Chiara, not in love with you. He doesn't know *how* to love. So take my advice and make sure that prenup of yours is ironclad."

"Duly noted," Chiara rasped, having had more than enough. "Now, if you'll excuse me, I need to find my *fiancé*."

Santo eyed Chiara as she stood toe-to-toe with Carolina. "Should we intercede?"

"Give it a minute," Lazzero murmured, eyes on the exchange. "Chiara can handle herself."

"That she can." Santo shifted his study back to him. "I remember now where I've seen her before. Chiara. She's the brunette you were chatting up at the *Score* premiere."

"I wasn't chatting her up," Lazzero corrected. "I was saying hello. Her friend won tickets to the launch. I see her every day—it would have been rude not to say hi."

His brother gave him a disbelieving look. "And you're trying to tell me she is all business? That all she does is make your espresso every morning? I don't believe it. Not with that body."

A flash of fire singed his belly. "Watch your words, Santo."

His brother blinked. "You *like* her."

"Of course I like her. I brought her with me."

"No, I mean, you *like* her. You've never once warned me off a woman like that."

"You're overthinking it."

"I think not." Santo gave him a considering look. "She is far from your usual type. I think your taste has improved."

It might have, Lazzero conceded, if Chiara were *his*. Which she was not.

Santo drained his glass as Chiara stalked through the crowd toward them, an infuriated look on her face. "I see a damsel in distress. Off to do my duty. Good luck with *that*."

Santo waltzed off into the crowd. Chiara slid onto the bar stool beside him, her green eyes flashing as she downed a gulp of champagne.

Lazzero eyed her. "What did she say?"

"She is—" Chiara waved a hand at him. "She was *rude*. She told me to make sure my prenup is airtight because it isn't going to last."

"It *isn't* going to last," he said. "This is fake, remember? Why are you so upset?"

She gave him a black look. "She made it clear a barista is *beneath* you."

"That's ridiculous."

"Is it?" Her mouth set in a mutinous line. "Carolina owns her own interior decorating firm. *I* am merely a barista you hired to play your fiancée...someone who couldn't, in a million years, afford to say no to your offer. Someone you would never *consider* marrying." Her eyes darkened. "This is exactly what I was talking about earlier...the games rich people play where people get hurt. Carolina might be a bitch, Lazzero, but she is *wounded*."

A flare of antagonism lanced through him. "I think you have it the wrong way around. I'm doing this so that *no one* gets hurt. If I made a mistake with Carolina, which I might have, it was in letting the relationship drag on for too long. Since I acknowledge I made that mistake, I am rectifying it now by not hurting her further by giving her hope for something that can never be."

She gave him a caustic look. "Exactly what do you think is going to happen if you do commit to a woman? The bogeyman is going to come get you?"

The fuse inside him caught fire. "Speaks the woman who doesn't date?"

"At least I acknowledge my faults."

"I just did," he growled. "And as far as you and Carolina are concerned, you are right, you are *not* in the same class as her. You *outclass* her in every way, Chiara. Carolina is an entitled piece of work who uses everything and everyone in her life to her own advantage. You are hardworking and fiercely independent with an honesty and integrity I admire. So can we please put the subject of your worth to rest?"

Her indignation came to a sliding halt. "So why *did* you date her, then?"

A hint of the devil arrowed through him, fueled by his intense irritation. "She took off her clothes during our consultation appointment at my penthouse. What was I going to do?"

Her eyes widened. "You aren't joking, are you?"

"No."

"I walked right into that one, didn't I?"

"Yes. Now," he murmured, bringing his mouth to her ear, "can we move on? Gianni just sat down at the end of the bar. He's watching us and I'd like to make this somewhat believable."

She blew out a breath. "Yes."

"Bene." He nodded toward her almost empty glass of champagne. "Drink up and let's dance."

She cast a wary eye toward the dance floor, where the couples were moving to the sinuous rhythm of a Latin tune. "Not to this."

"This," he insisted, sliding off the stool and tugging her off hers.

"Lazzero, I don't know how," she protested, setting her glass on the bar and dragging her feet. "It's been years since I took salsa lessons and I was *terrible*. I'm going to look ridiculous out there."

He stopped on the edge of the dance floor and tipped her chin up with his fingers. "All you have to do is let me lead," he said softly. "Give up that formidable control of yours for once, Chiara, because this dance doesn't work without complete and total…submission."

Chiara's heart thumped wildly against her ribs as Lazzero led her onto the dance floor. The feel of his fingers wrapped around her wrist sent a surge of electricity through her, tiny sparks unearthing themselves over every inch of her skin.

This is such a bad, bad idea.

A new song began as they found a free space among the dancers. Sultry and seductive, it brought back memories of the bruised feet and embarrassing silences she'd stumbled through in dance classes. She attempted one last objection as Lazzero pulled her close, clasping one hand around hers, the other resting against her back. "Back on one," he said, cutting off her protest, "forward on five."

She wasn't sure how she was supposed to remember the *first* step with the heat of his tall, muscular body so close to hers, his sexy, spicy aftershave infiltrating her head. But she couldn't just stand there on the dance floor doing nothing with everyone watching, so she took a deep breath and stepped back to mirror Lazzero's basic step.

Her lessons, remarkably, came back immediately, the basic step easy enough to execute. Except she was all out of rhythm and stumbled into him, her cheeks heating.

"Follow my lead," Lazzero growled. "And look at *me*, not at the floor. When I push, you step back, when I pull, you move forward. It's very basic. Follow my signals."

Except that was a dangerous thing to do because his eyes had a sexy, seductive glimmer in them that had nothing to do with a business deal and the champagne had now fully gone to her head, making any attempt at sophisticated steps a concerted effort.

Forcing herself to concentrate, she followed his lead before she fell flat on her face. His grip firm and commanding, he guided her through the steps until she was picking out the basic movement in time to the music.

"Now you've got it," he murmured, as they executed a simple right turn. "See, isn't this fun?"

It was, in fact, with a lead as good as Lazzero. He moved in ways a man shouldn't be able to, his hips fluid and graceful. She started to trust he would place her where she needed to be and gave herself in to the sensual rhythm of the dance. The champagne, fully charging her bloodstream now, had the positive effect of loosening her inhibitions even further as they pulled off some more sophisticated steps and turns.

By the time the song was over, she was having so much fun, she fell laughing into Lazzero's arms on the final turn. Caught up in all that muscle, his powerful body pressed against the length of hers, she swallowed past the racing of her heart as a languorous, slow number began to play. "Maybe we should go get a drink," she suggested, breathlessly. "I am *seriously* thirsty."

"While I have you so soft and compliant and all womanly in my arms?" he mocked lightly, sliding an arm around her waist to pull her closer. "We're actually managing to be convincing at the moment. I'd like to enjoy the novelty before the arrows start flying again."

"I don't do that," she protested.

"Yes, you do." He gave her a considering look. "I think it's a defense mechanism."

"Against what?"

"I'm still trying to figure that out."

She followed him through the slow, lazy steps, excruciatingly aware of the hard press of his powerful thighs against hers, the thump of his heart beneath her hand, *the brush of his mouth against her temple.*

"Lazzero," she breathed.

"The Casales are watching. Relax."

Impossible. Not with the warm touch of those sensual lips on her skin giving her an idea of how they'd feel all over her. The smooth caress of his palm against the small of her back, burning into her bare skin. Definitely not when his mouth traced a path along the length of her jaw.

He was going to kiss her, she registered with a wild jump of her heart. And there was nothing she could do to stop it. Nor could she even pretend she wanted to.

Electric shivers slid up her spine as he tilted her chin up with his thumb, holding her captive to his purposeful ebony gaze. Her breath stopped in her chest as he bent his head and lowered his mouth to hers in a butterfly-light kiss meant to seduce.

This isn't real, she cautioned herself. But it was fruitless, as every nerve ending seemed to catch fire. Lips whispering against hers, his thumb stroking her jaw, he teased and tantalized with so much sensual expertise, she was lost before the battle even began, her lips clinging to his as she tentatively returned the kiss.

Nestling her jaw more securely in his palm, he tugged her up on tiptoe with the hand he held at her waist and took the kiss deeper. Head tilted back, each slide of his mouth over hers sending sparks through her, Chiara forgot everything but what it felt like to be kissed like this. To be *seduced.* As if lightning had struck.

A sound left the back of her throat as her fingers crept around his neck. Clenched tensile, hard muscle. Murmuring his approval, he nudged her mouth apart with the slick glide of his tongue and delved inside with a heated caress that liquefied her insides. Weakened her knees.

She moved closer to him, wanting, *needing* his support. His hand slid to her hip, shifting her closer to all that muscle, until she was molded to every centimeter of him, the languorous drift of his mouth over hers, his deep, drugging kisses, shooting sparks of fire through her.

A low groan tore itself from his throat, the hand he held at her bottom bringing her into direct contact with the shockingly hard ridge of his arousal. She should have been scandalized. Instead, the wave of heat coursing through her crashed deeper, a fission of white-hot sexual awareness arcing through her.

She was so far gone, so lost in him, she almost protested when Lazzero broke the kiss with a nuzzling slowness, his fingers at her waist holding her steady as he dragged his mouth to her ear.

"The song is over," he murmured. "As much as I hate to say it."

The lazy satisfaction in his voice, the beat of a fast new tune, brought the world into focus with shocking swiftness. *What was she doing? Had she lost her mind?* Lazzero had kissed her to prove a point to the Casales. This was just a *game* to him, she simply a pawn he was playing. And she had pretty much thrown herself at him.

Head spinning, heart pounding, she pulled herself out of his arms. "Chiara," he murmured, his eyes on hers, "it was just a kiss."

Just a kiss. It felt as if the earth had moved beneath her feet. Like nothing she'd ever experienced before, not even with Antonio who'd been practiced in the art of seduction. But for Lazzero, it had been *just a kiss.*

Had she learned nothing from her experiences?

She took a step back. Lifted her chin. "*Sì,*" she agreed unsteadily, "it was just a kiss. And, now that we've given an award-winning performance, I think I've had enough."

CHAPTER FIVE

JUST A KISS.

Clearly, Lazzero conceded as he drove back to the hotel at the close of the night, that hadn't been the right line to feed Chiara at that particular moment in time. She had given him one of those death glares of hers, stalked off the dance floor and remained distant for the rest of the evening, unless required to turn it on for public consumption.

The chill had continued in the car, with her blowing off his attempts at conversation. But could he blame her, really? A kiss might have been in order, but *that* hadn't been necessary. That had been pure self-gratification on his part.

He should have stopped it before it had gotten hot enough to melt the two of them to the dance floor. Before he'd confirmed what he'd always known about them—that they would be ridiculously, spectacularly hot together. But Chiara's unwarranted, unfair judgments of him had burrowed beneath his skin. And, if he were being honest, so had his need to prove he was not the *last* man on earth she'd ever want, he was *the* one she wanted.

His curiosity about what it would be like to strip away those formidable defenses of hers had been irresistible. To find the passion that lay beneath. And hell, had he found it.

His blood thickened at the memory of her sweet, sensual response. It had knocked him sideways, the feel of those lush, amazing curves beneath his hands as good as he'd imagined they would be. He'd let the kiss get way out of hand, no doubt about it, but he hadn't been the only participant.

Chiara was out of the car and on her way into the lobby as he handed the keys to the Lamborghini to the valet, shocking him with how swiftly she could walk in those insanely high shoes. She had jammed her finger on the call button for the elevator by the time he'd made it into the lobby, her toe tapping impatiently on the marble. It came seconds later and swished them silently up to the third floor.

Kicking off her shoes in the marble foyer of the penthouse, she continued her relentless path through the living room, into the bedroom. He caught up with her before she reached the bathroom door. Curved a hand around her arm. "Chiara," he murmured. "We need to talk."

She swung around, a closed look on her face. "About what? You were right, Lazzero, it was *just a kiss*. And now, if you don't mind, I am going to go to bed. I am exhausted." Her eyes lifted mutinously to his. "*If* I am *off duty*, of course."

Oh, no. Red misted his vision as she pulled out of his grasp and stalked into the bathroom, slamming the door in his face. She wasn't going to go there.

Walk away, he told himself. Shake it off. Deal with this tomorrow when saner heads prevail.

Except nothing about that kiss had been business and they both knew it. It had been a long time coming, *a year* precisely, since he'd walked through the door of the Daily Grind and found Chiara cursing at an espresso machine on a particularly bad day. They *had* something. That was clear. They were consenting adults. What the hell was the problem?

He stalked into the dressing room. Threw his wallet and change on the armoire. The wounded look on Chiara's face in the car filtered through his head. She thought he was playing with her. That this was a *game* to him. Which, admittedly it might have started out as, until he'd gotten as caught up in that kiss as she had been.

Leaving her to stew, he decided as he stripped off his bow tie and cuff links, was not a good idea. Tossing them on the dresser, he rapped on the bedroom door. Walked in. Frowned when he found the room empty, the bed untouched. Then he spotted Chiara on the balcony, her back to him.

Definitely stewing.

He crossed to the French doors. Stopped in his tracks. She was dressed for bed, a factor he hadn't taken into consideration. Which needed to be taken into consideration, because what she was wearing heated his blood.

The simple tank top and shorts were hardly the sexiest nightwear he'd ever seen, covering more of her than most women did on the streets of Manhattan. It was the way the soft jersey material clung to her voluptuous body that made his mouth go dry.

His hands itched to touch, to give in to the craving he'd been fighting all night, but he stayed where he was, framed in the light of the suite.

"It wasn't just a kiss."

His quiet words had Chiara spinning around. An equally spectacular view from the front, he noted, her face bare of makeup, lush mouth pursed in contemplation, her legs a sweep of smooth golden skin that seemed to go on forever.

He set his gaze on hers. "That kiss was spectacular. You and I both know it. I wanted to do it since the first moment I saw you in that dress tonight. Actually," he amended huskily, "since the first day I set eyes on you in the coffee shop. You and I have something, Chiara. It would be ridiculous to deny it."

She swallowed hard, the delicate muscles in her throat

convulsing. A myriad of emotion flickered through her green eyes. "You were toying with me, Lazzero."

He shook his head. "I was satisfying my *curiosity* about the attraction between us. Finding out how it would be. And you were curious too," he added deliberately, eyeing the flare of awareness staining her olive skin. "But you won't admit it, because you're so intent on protecting yourself, on preserving that prickly outer layer of yours, on putting your *labels* on me, you won't admit how you feel."

A fiery light stormed her eyes. "You're damn right I am. I have no interest in becoming your latest conquest, Lazzero. In being bought with a piece of jewelry. In performing ever greater circus tricks to retain your interest, only to be dumped in a cloud of dust when I no longer do. I have *been there* and *done that*."

His jaw dropped. "That's absurd."

"You said it at Di Fiore's. Your relationships only last as long as your interest does." She planted her hands on her hips. "The soul-baring truth and nothing but. Isn't that how you put it?"

He had no response for that, grounded by his own transparency. She tipped her chin up. "Consider my curiosity well and truly satisfied. My *list* ticked off."

His ego took that stunning blow as she turned and stalked inside, effectively ending the conversation. Except which part of it hadn't been true? He was all of that and more.

He followed her inside, stripped off his clothes in the guest bathroom and deposited himself under a chilly shower to cool his body down, still revved up from that almost-sex on the dance floor.

He played by a certain set of rules because that's what he was capable of. He was never going to allow a woman *in*, was never going to commit, because he knew the destructive force a relationship could be. He'd watched his father wind himself in circles over his mother before he'd imploded in spectacular fashion, a roller coaster ride he was never getting on. Ever.

Getting his head tied up in Chiara, no matter how hot he was for her, was insanity with everything riding on this deal with Gianni. He'd best keep that in mind or *he* was going to be the one going down in a cloud of dust.

Pulling on boxer shorts in deference to his company, he braced himself for the far-too-short-looking sofa in the bedroom, the only sleepable surface in the suite other than the extremely comfortable-looking four-poster bed. Which was...*empty*.

What the hell?

He found Chiara curled up on the sofa, a blanket covering her slight form. Her dark hair spread out like silk against the white pillowcase, long, decadent lashes fanned down against her cheeks, she was deep asleep.

Every male instinct growled in irritation. This had clearly been her parting volley. *Clearly*, she didn't know him well enough if she thought he was going to let her sleep there, no matter how amazing that bed looked after the couple of hours of sleep he'd had on the plane.

Moving silently across the room, he slid his arms beneath her, lifted her up and carried her to the bed. Transferring her weight to one arm, he tossed the silk comforter aside and slid her into the bed. She was so deep asleep she didn't blink an eyelash as she shifted onto her stomach and burrowed into the silk sheets. Which gave him a very tantalizing view of her amazing derriere in the feminine shorts.

The reminder of what those curves had felt like beneath his hands, how perfectly she'd fit against him, sizzled the blood in his veins. Revved him up all over again. A low curse leaving his throat, he retreated to the sofa, flicked the blanket aside and settled his hormone-ravaged body onto the ridiculous excuse for a piece of furniture.

His attempts to get comfortable were futile. When he stretched out, his feet hung over the edge, cutting off his circulation. When he attempted to contort himself to fit, his old basketball injury made his knee throb.

The minutes ticked by, his need to sleep growing ever more acute. He had four hours maximum before he had to get up for his practice with a team of world-class athletes who were going to run him into the ground at this rate. He must have been insane to agree to play.

He had shifted positions for what must have been the tenth time when Chiara lifted herself up on her elbow and blinked at him in the darkness. "How did I get into the bed?"

"I carried you there," he said grumpily. "Go back to sleep."

She dropped back to the pillow. A silence followed. Then a drowsy, "Get in the bed, Lazzero. It's as big as Milan. We can share it."

He was off the sofa and in the bed in record time. It *was* the size of Milan and he could restrain himself. Finding a comfortable position on the far side of the bed, he closed his eyes and lost himself to blissful unconsciousness.

Chiara was having the most delicious dream. Plastered against a wall of heat, she was warm and cocooned and thoroughly content after finding the air-conditioning distinctly chilly during the night.

Pressing closer to all that heat, she registered it was hot, hard muscle—hot, hard *male* muscle that was its source. Utterly in tune with the whole picture because she had truly outdone herself with this dream, she pressed even closer.

A big, warm hand slid over the curve of her hip to arrange her more comfortably on top of him. She sighed and went willingly, because he felt deliciously good against her, underneath her, *everywhere*, and it had been so long, so damn long since she'd been touched like this. *Held* like this.

He traced his fingers down her spine, savoring the texture and shape of her. She purred like a cat and arched into him. The sensual slide of his mouth against the delicate skin of her throat stirred her pulse to a drumbeat. Melted her insides. A shiver coursing through her, she turned her head to find the kiss he was offering. *Best dream ever.*

Slow, lazy, decadent, it was perfection. She moved closer still, wanting more. His hand closed possessively over her bottom, a low sound of male pleasure reverberating against her mouth.

Too real.

Oh, my God.

She broke the kiss. Sank her palms into his rock-hard chest, panic arrowing through her as she stared into Lazzero's sleepy, slumberous gaze. Registered the palm he held against her back, the other that cupped her buttock, plastering her against him, exactly as she'd been in her dream.

Except it hadn't been a dream. It had been real. *Good God.*

She pushed frantically against his chest. Scrambled off him. Lazzero eyed her lazily, his ebony eyes blinking awake. "What's the hurry?" he murmured, his husky, sleep-infused voice rumbling down her spine. "That was one hell of a way to wake a man up, *caro.*"

She sat back on her heels. Ran a shaky hand through her hair. "You took advantage of the situation."

"I think you have that the wrong way around," he drawled. "I have been on this side of the bed all night, a fact I made damn sure of. Which means it was *you* who found your way over here." He lifted a brow. "Maybe it was your subconscious talking after that kiss last night?"

Her cheeks fired. "I had no idea *who* I was kissing."

He crossed his arms over his chest and lounged back

against the pillows. "Funny that, because you sighed my name. Twice. I'm fairly sure that's what woke me up."

She searched his face for some sign he was joking. "I did *not*."

His smug expression gave her little hope. She dropped her gaze away from his, utterly disconcerted, but that was an even bigger problem because he was jaw dropping— perfectly hewn, bronzed muscle, marred only by the scar that crisscrossed his knee. Better than she could ever have imagined, his low-slung boxers did little to hide his potent masculinity. Which was more than a little stirred up at the moment. *By her.*

"I am," he murmured, pulling her gaze back up to his, "wide-awake now, on the other hand, if you are looking for my full participation."

Her stomach swooped. Searching desperately for sanity, she shimmied across the massive bed and slid off it. Felt the heat of Lazzero's gaze follow her, burning over the exposed length of her legs. "I need to shower," she announced, heading for the bathroom as fast as her legs would carry her.

"Coward," he tossed after her.

She kept going. He could call her what he liked. If she didn't get her head on her shoulders, figure out how to wrangle her attraction to Lazzero under control, she was going to mess this up, because this was *not* her world and she was hopelessly out of her depth. And since messing this up was not an option, she needed to restore her common sense. *Yesterday.*

Joining the other girlfriends, wives and friends of the players in the VIP seating area at San Siro stadium for the practice proved to offer plenty of opportunity for Chiara to recover her composure. It was packed with women in designer outfits and expensive perfume, sophisticated perfection she couldn't hope to emulate.

Dressed in a pair of white capri jeans and a fuchsia-colored blouse she had knotted at the waist, a cute pair of white sneakers on her feet, she looked the part, but how could she possibly participate in the conversations going on around her? What did she know about Cannes for the film festival or an annual Easter weekend on a Russian oligarch's yacht?

She found herself confined to the outer fringe of the group, the cold shoulder Carolina had given her instigating that phenomenon, no doubt. She wasn't sure why she cared. This wasn't her world, she didn't want it to be her world. But that didn't mean it didn't hurt. That it didn't remind her of the mean girls in school who'd ridiculed her for her hopelessly out-of-date, out-of-fashion clothes.

Putting on the aloof face she'd perfected in school, she positioned herself at the end of the bleacher, pretending not to care. The lovely, bubbly wife of the Western European team captain, Valentino Calabria, sat down beside her, dragging one of the other wives with her as she braved the cold front. "Don't pay any attention to them," Pia Calabria murmured. "It takes years to break into their clique."

Pia kept up a continual stream of conversation as the Americas team took to the field for its practice, for which Chiara was inordinately grateful. It was hard, brutal play as the team geared up for its opening match against Western Europe, sweat and curses flying.

Pia sat back as the play halted for a water break, fanning her face with her purse. "The eye candy," she pronounced with a dramatic sigh, "is simply too much for me to handle today."

"Which you are not supposed to be noticing with Valentino, the *magnifico*, right in front of you," Pia's friend reprimanded drily.

Pia slid her a sideways look. "And you are not doing the same? *Looking* is not a crime."

Chiara's gaze moved to Lazzero. It *was* impossible not to ogle. Intense and compelling in black shorts and a sweaty, bright green Americas T-shirt, he looked amazing.

"Him," Pia agreed, following her gaze to Lazzero, who stood in the middle of the field, wiping the sweat off his forehead with the hem of his T-shirt as he yelled at his teammates to get ready for the kick in. "Exactly. Now, there is a *man*. Those abs… You could bounce a football off of them. And those thighs…" She rolled her eyes heavenward. "*Insano*. No wonder Carolina is going ballistic."

Chiara kept her eyes glued to the field. Thought about that ridiculously amazing kiss she'd shared with Lazzero that morning. It had felt undeniably *right*. As if she and Lazzero had something, exactly as he'd said. She would be lying if she said she wasn't desperately curious to know what it would have been like if she'd let it play out to its seductive conclusion, because she knew it would have been incredible.

You're a senior citizen at twenty-six. Kat's jibe flitted tauntingly through her head. Her life *was* pathetic. She *had* no life. But to take a walk on the wild side with Lazzero, who'd surely annihilate her before it was all over? It seemed patently unwise.

She pushed her attention back to the field, rather than allow it to continue down the ridiculous road it was traveling. Watched as Lazzero's squad executed an impressive series of passes to put the ball in the net.

"Hell." Pia covered her eyes. "They look good. Too good. Valentino is going to be unbearable if they lose."

The practice ended shortly thereafter. Chiara dutifully engaged a cool Carolina in a stilted conversation as she'd promised Lazzero she would so that he could catch up with Gianni before the sponsor lunch. When Carolina blew her off a few minutes later, she found herself at loose ends as Pia drifted off to find her husband.

Giving her father a quick call at the bakery before he began work, she assured herself he was okay, then got up to stretch her legs and go look for Lazzero when some of the Americas team players started to drift back onto the field. Heading toward the tunnel where the players were coming out, she stopped dead in her tracks at the sight of Lazzero and Carolina engaged in conversation in the shadowed passage. Carolina, stunning in a bright yellow dress, was leaning against the wall, Lazzero standing in front of her, his head bent close to hers, his hand on the wall beside her.

Intimate, *familiar*, the conversation looked intense. Sharp claws dragged through her. What were they talking about? Was Carolina trying to convince Lazzero she would leave Gianni for him? She had no doubt the other woman would do so in a flash, more than a bit in love with him still.

The jealousy that rocketed through her was illogical, she knew it. She and Lazzero were putting on a charade. It *wasn't* real. But the visceral emotion sweeping through her was.

She swung away, her insides coiling. Walked into a brick wall. She looked up to find Lucca Sousa, the celebrated Brazilian captain of the Americas' squad steadying her, his hands at her waist. Glancing down the tunnel, Lucca absorbed the scene she'd just witnessed, a frown creasing his brow.

"Nothing to see there," he murmured, pressing a hand to her back and guiding her away from the tunnel. "Ancient history, that is."

It hadn't looked so ancient. It had looked very *present*.

"At loose ends?" Lucca queried, giving the group of football wives a glance.

Chiara shot him a distracted look. "I am not part of their clique."

"Nor do you want to be," he said firmly. "Take it from me. Come—kick a ball around with me before lunch."

He was taking pity on her, she registered, a low burn of humiliation moving through her. Helping her save face. It unearthed a wound she'd buried layers deep, because she knew what it was like to be the side amusement for a man who had more than his fair share of willing participants.

But tall, dark and gorgeous Lucca, as smooth as Lazzero was hard around the edges, refused to take no for an answer. Procuring a ball from the sidelines, he ignored his own personal posse lining up to talk to him and shepherded Chiara onto the field. "Do you play?"

She shook her head. "Only a bit in school."

"That will do." Giving her an instruction to move back a few feet, they dribbled the ball back and forth. A couple of the other players and their wives joined in and they played a minigame at one end of the field, a crowd gathering to watch the good-natured fun. Lucca and she proved decent partners, mainly because he was brilliant and as patient as the end of the day.

Chiara, who hadn't been a bad player in school, still found the precision required to get the ball in the net exceedingly frustrating, particularly after all this time. Lucca stopped the play, moved behind her and guided her through the motion of an accurate, straight kick. It took her a few tries, but finally she seemed to master it.

They played the game to five, Chiara's confidence growing as they went. When their team won the game, she jumped in the air in victory. Lucca trotted over and gave her a big hug, lifting her off her feet. "Don't look now," he murmured, glancing at the sidelines, "but your fiancé is watching and he looks, how do I say it in English...*chateado*. Pissed."

Cheeks flushed, exhilarated from the exercise, she stood on tiptoe and gave him a kiss on the cheek, knowing she was stoking the fire, but unable to help herself. "Thank you. That was so much fun."

"You're good at this," Lucca drawled, his eyes sparkling. "Go get him."

Her stomach turned inside out as she walked off the field toward Lazzero, who was standing on the sidelines, dressed in dark jeans and a shirt, arms crossed over his chest.

"Should we go in to lunch?" she suggested coolly when she reached his side. "It looks like it's ready."

"In a minute." He shoved his hands into his jean pockets, his gaze resting on hers. Combustible. *Distinctly combustible.* "Having fun?" he asked.

"Actually, yes, I was. Lucca is lovely."

"He's the biggest playboy on that side of the Atlantic, Chiara."

"I thought that was you," she returned sweetly.

"He had his hands all over you," he murmured. "We are supposed to be newly engaged—madly in love. You might try giving that impression."

Her chin came up, heat coursing through her. "Maybe *you* shouldn't be canoodling with your ex, then. Everyone saw you, Lazzero. You're lucky Gianni didn't."

He raked a hand through his hair. "Carolina was upset. I was doing damage control."

"So was I. If people were watching Lucca and I, then they weren't watching you. And honestly," she purred, "I don't think there is a woman on the planet who would object to having Lucca Sousa's hands on her, so really, it was no hardship. You can thank me later."

His gaze darkened. "Trying to push my buttons, Chiara?"

She lifted a brow. "Now, why would I do that? This isn't real, after all."

Lazzero attempted to douse his incendiary mood with a cold beer at lunch as he sat through the interminably long, posturing event with all its requisite speeches and small

talk. The urge to connect his fist with Lucca Sousa's undeniably handsome jaw was potently appealing. Which was
not a rational response, but then again, Chiara seemed to
inspire that particular frame of mind in him.

His black mood might also, he conceded, be attributed
to Gianni. He'd finally pinned the Italian CEO down before lunch, but their conversation had not been the one he'd
been looking for.

He finessed an escape as dessert ran into ever-lasting
coffee, promising to meet Chiara at the exit once he'd collected his things. Packing his things up, he ran into Santo
on his way out of the locker room.

His brother's eyes gleamed with amusement as he rested
a palm against the frame of the door. "Everything under
control with your fiery little barista? You look a bit hot
under the collar."

"Not now, Santo." Lazzero moved into the hallway for
some privacy. "I talked to Gianni."

Santo lifted a brow. "How did it go?"

"Not great," he admitted. "He seems to have some reservations about how the two brands will work together. If
our design philosophies will match. But he wasn't saying
no. He wants to meet on Tuesday."

"Well that's something." Santo shrugged. "Show him
the design ideas we've developed. They're impressive."

Lazzero shook his head. "Those designs are all wrong.
I'm not happy with them."

A wary look claimed his brother's face. "This is not the
time for your obsessive perfectionism, Laz. The designs
are fine. *Use them.* We might not get another crack at him."

"We definitely won't if we use those drawings," Lazzero
said flatly. "Gianni will hate them. I *know* him. We need
him on board, Santo."

Heat flared in his brother's eyes. "I am clear on that. *I,*
however, wasn't the one who decided to go off half-cocked

on the annual investor call and tell the world we're going to be the number two sportswear brand when number three was a stretch."

A red haze enveloped his brain. "That damn analyst led me on, Santo. You know she did. She loves to push me."

"And *you* shouldn't have bitten. But that's irrelevant now. *Now* we have to deliver. We go back empty-handed and the financial community will crucify us." His brother fixed his gaze on his. "We both know how fast a rising star can crash, Laz. How it's all about perception. What happens if we start to look as if we've overshot our orbit."

Broken, irreparable dreams and all the inherent destruction that comes with it.

His father had been one of the greatest deal-makers on Wall Street—a risk-taking rainmaker who had made a fortune for his clients. Until he'd taken the biggest risk of all, founded a company of his own on a belief those riches could be his, and lost everything.

He *knew* the dangers in making promises you couldn't keep. In trying to grow a company too far, too fast. Had grown up with its repercussions falling down around him, just as Santo and Nico had. But he also knew his instincts weren't wrong on Volare.

"You need to trust me. We have *always* trusted each other. I can do this, Santo. I can make us number two. You just need to give me the room to maneuver."

His brother studied him for a long moment, his dark gaze conflicted. "I do trust you," he said finally. "That's my problem, Laz. I'm not sure if this obsessive drive of yours is going to make us or break us."

"It's going to make us," Lazzero said. *"Trust me."*

CHAPTER SIX

LAZZERO EMERGED FROM the luxurious office space at the Orientale at close to midnight, having spent the evening consulting with his design team in New York, attempting to come up with some sketches for Gianni that worked. An effort which had not yet yielded fruit, but *had* achieved his dual purpose of staying away from Chiara and his inexplicable inability to control himself when it came to her.

Tracing a silent path through the living room to the bedroom, he found the rumpled bed unoccupied and light pooling into the room from the terrace. Crossing to the French doors, he found Chiara curled up on the sofa, staring out at an unparalleled view of Milan. The moon cast an ethereal glow over the beautiful, aristocratic city, but it was Chiara's face that held his attention—the stark vulnerability written across those lush, expressive features, the quiet stillness about her that said she was in another place entirely.

Dressed in the silky, feminine shorts and tank top she seemed to favor, her hair rumpled from sleep, she looked about eighteen. Except there was nothing youthful about the body underneath that wistful packaging. The fine material of her top hugged every last centimeter of her perfect breasts, her hips a voluptuous, irresistible curve beneath the shorts that left her long, golden legs bare.

His blood turned to fire, his good intentions incinerating on a wave of lust that threatened to annihilate his common sense. *So he had a thing for her. Maybe he had a gigantic thing for her. He could control it.*

Maybe if he kept telling himself that, he'd actually believe it.

She turned to look at him, as if sensing his presence. The emotion he read in her brilliant green eyes rocked him back on his heels. It was impossible to decipher—too mixed and too complex, but he could sense a yearning behind it and it turned a key inside of him. Melted that common sense away into so much dust.

"Did you get your designs figured out?" Her voice was husky from lack of use.

He shook his head. "The team's still working on it." He picked up the hardback book she had sitting beside her, a pencil tucked into the binding, and sat down. "You couldn't sleep?"

"My head was too full."

With what? He looked down at the book he held, a sketchbook of some sort, open to a drawing of a dress. "What's this?"

"Nothing. It's just a hobby. I like to make my own clothes." She reached for the book, but he held on to it and flipped through the sketches.

"These are really good. Do you have formal training?"

"I did a few semesters of a fashion design degree at Parsons."

"Only a few semesters?" He directed an inquisitive gaze at her. "It's one of the best design programs in the country. Why did you stop?"

"We needed to prioritize money for the bakery." She shrugged. "It was a long shot anyway."

"Says who? Parsons clearly thought you had talent."

Her expression took on a closed edge. "The program was insanely competitive—the design career I would have had even more so. It just wasn't realistic."

He snapped the book shut and handed it to her. "The best things in life are the hardest to attain. What was the end goal if you'd continued with your degree? To go work for a designer?"

She shook her head. "I wanted to create my own line of affordable urban fashion."

"A big dream," he conceded. "What was your inspiration for it?"

She drew her knees up to her chest and rested her head against the back of the sofa. "My mother," she said, a wistful look in her eyes. "We didn't have much growing up. The bakery did okay, but there was no room for extras. My father considered fashion a luxury, not a necessity, which meant I wore cheap, department store clothes or my cousin's hand-me-downs. Hard," she acknowledged, "for a teenage girl trying to fit in with the cool crowd.

"Thankfully, my mother was an excellent seamstress. After dinner, when the bakery was closed, she'd brew a pot of tea, we'd spread the patterns out on the floor and make the clothes I wanted." A smile curved her lips. "She was incredible. She could make anything. It was magical to me, the way the pieces came together. There was never any doubt as to what I wanted to be."

"And then she passed away," Lazzero murmured.

"Yes. My father, he was—" she hesitated, searching for the right words "—he was never really the same after my mother's death. He was dark, *lost*. He worshipped the ground she walked on. All he seemed to know how to do was to keep the bakery going—to *provide*. But I wouldn't go out with my friends, because of how dark he would get. I was worried about what he would do—what he *might* do. So, I stayed home and took care of him. Made my own clothes. It became a form of self-expression for me."

His heart contracted, the echoes of an ancient wound pulsing his insides. "He was angry. Not at you—at the disease. For taking your mother from him. For shattering his life."

Her dark lashes fanned her cheeks. "You were like that with your father."

He nodded. The difference was, his father's disease had been preventable. Perhaps even more difficult to accept.

Chiara returned her gaze to the glittering city view. "Designing became my obsession. My way of countering the mean girls at school who made fun of my clothes. My lack of designer labels. Sometimes I would make things from scratch, other times I would buy pieces from the thrift store and alter them—not to follow the trends but to reflect what *I* loved about fashion. Eventually," she allowed, "those girls wanted me to make things for them."

"And did you? After what they'd done?"

She nodded.

"Why?"

"Because anger doesn't solve anything," she said quietly. "Only forgiveness does. Allowing my designs to speak for me."

Lazzero felt something stick in his chest. That struck him as phenomenal—*she* struck him as phenomenal—that she would have that sense of maturity, wisdom, at such a young age.

But hadn't he? It was a trait you developed when you were left to fend for yourself. *Sink or swim. Protect yourself at all costs. Arm yourself against the world.* But unlike Chiara, he had had his brothers. She'd had no one.

For the first time he wondered how, in withdrawing when his mother had left, retreating into that aloof, unknowable version of himself he did so well, what effect that had had on his brothers. What it must have been like for Nico, at fifteen, to leave school, to abandon the dreams he'd had for himself to take care of him and Santo. How selflessly he'd done it. How Chiara had had none of that support and turned out to be as strong as she was.

He picked up her hand and tugged it into his lap. Marveled at how small and delicate it was. At the voltage that came from touching her, the connection between them an invisible, electrical thread that lit up his insides in the most dangerous of ways.

"You need to go back to school," he murmured. "Defeating the mean girls was your mission statement in life, Chiara. Some people search a lifetime for one. You *have* one. If you quit—*they* win."

Her gaze clouded over. "That ship has sailed. My classmates are done and building their careers. I'm too old to start again now."

His mouth twisted. "You're only twenty-six. You have plenty of time."

"Speaks the man who put Supersonic on the Nasdaq by the time he was twenty-five."

He shook his head. "You can't compare yourself to others. Santo and I had Martino, our godfather, to back us. To *guide* us. And Nico, who is every bit as brilliant."

She slanted him a curious look. "Was Martino family? What was the relationship between him and your father?"

He shook his head. "Martino and my father were on Wall Street together. Two of the biggest names in their day. Intense competitors and the best of friends."

"Was that where your father's alcoholism began? I've heard stories about the pressure...the crazy lifestyle."

"It started there," he acknowledged. "My father was levelheaded. Smart. Just like Martino. They both swore they'd get out once they'd made their money. Martino, true to his word, did. He founded Evolution with his wife, Juliette, and the rest is history. My father, however, got sucked into the lifestyle. The *temptations* of it.

"My mother," he continued, "didn't make it easier for

him by taking full advantage of that lifestyle and spending his money as if it were water. When Martino finally convinced my father to leave, he was intent on proving he could do it bigger and better than Martino. He bet the bank and his entire life savings on a technology start-up he and a client founded that never made it off the ground."

"And lost everything." Chiara's eyes glittered as they rested on his.

"Yes."

"Did Martino try and help your father? To pull him out of it?"

His mouth flattened. "He tried everything." *Just as they had.* Pouring bottles down the sink. Hiding them. Destroying them. Nico walking their father to AA every night before he'd gone to evening classes. None of it had worked.

Chiara watched him with those expressive eyes. "When did Martino take you under his wing?"

"After my father's funeral. My father was too humiliated to have anything to do with Martino when he was alive. Martino had conquered where he had failed. He refused all help from him. They had," he conceded, staring up at the scattering of stars that dotted the midnight sky, "a complex relationship as you can imagine."

Chiara didn't reply. He looked over at her, found her lost in thought. "What?"

She shrugged a slim shoulder. "I just— I wonder—" She sighed. "Sometimes I wonder if that's why my father withdrew after my mother died. Because I reminded him too much of her. We were mirror images, she and I."

"No." He squashed that imagining dead with a squeeze of his fingers around hers. "You can't take that on. People who are mired in grief get caught up in their own pain. It's as if they're in so deep, they can't dig their way out. They try," he acknowledged, "but it's as if they've made it to the other side, they're clawing their way to the surface, but they can't make it those last few feet to get out."

Her eyes grew dark. "Your father couldn't climb out?"

He nodded. And for the first time in his life, he realized how angry he was. How furious he was that his father who had always been superhuman in his eyes, his *hero*, hadn't had the strength to kick a disease that had destroyed his childhood. How angry he was that, in his supreme selfishness, his father had put his grief above *them*. At those who had created such a culture of reckless greed, his father had been unable to resist, tempted by sirens he didn't have the strength or desire to fight.

"You can't blame yourself," he told her. "This is about your father's inability to put you first, which he *should* have done."

"He did in a financial sense," Chiara pointed out.

"But you needed the emotional support, as well. That's just as important to a fifteen-year-old. And that, he didn't give you."

She sank her teeth into her lip. "Maybe I didn't give him what he needed, either. He was so lost. I didn't know what to do. I keep thinking maybe if I'd gotten him some help, if I'd done *something*, he wouldn't be the way he is. As if he's half-alive. As if he'd rather not be."

Her eyes glittered with tears, unmistakable diamond-edged drops that tugged hard at his insides. The defiant tilt of her chin annihilated his willpower completely. "Chiara," he murmured, pulling her into his arms, his chin coming down on top of her head, her petite body curved against his, "this is not on you. It's about him. You can't find his happiness for him. He has to find it himself."

"And what if he doesn't?"

"Then you were there for him. That's all you can do."

He thought she might pull out of his arms then, a pal-pable tension in her slight frame. Which would have been the smart move given the chemistry that pulsed between them. Instead, heaving a sigh, she curled closer. Her jasmine-scented hair soft as silk against his skin, the silent, dark night wrapping itself around them, it was a fit so perfect, his brain struggled to articulate it. For once in his life, he didn't even try.

His mouth whispered against the delicate curve of her jaw in an attempt to comfort. The rasp of his stubble against her satiny skin raked a shiver through her. Through *him*.

She went perfectly still. As if she'd forgotten how to move, how to breathe. His palm anchored against her back, her softness pressed against his hardness, his brain slid back to that lazy, sexy kiss this morning. The leisurely, undoubtedly mind-blowing conclusion he would have taken it to if it had been his call.

His blood thickened in his veins, his self-imposed celibacy over the past few months slamming into him hard. His fingers on her jaw, he turned her face to his. Her dark lashes glistening with unshed tears, her lush mouth bare of color, the flare of sensual awareness that darkened her beautiful green eyes was unmistakable. The kind that invited a man to jump in and drown himself in it.

Vulnerable. Too vulnerable.

"Lazzero," she murmured.

This isn't happening.

He lifted her up and carried her inside. In one deft move, he sank his fingers beneath the silky hair at her nape and whisked his arm from beneath her thighs until she slid down his body to her feet, the rasp of her ripe curves against his sensitized flesh almost sending him up into flames.

He doused the vicious heat with a bucketful of cold determination. Because this, *this* could not happen right now. His brain was far too full and she was too damn fragile.

He reached up to tuck a rumpled tendril of her hair behind her ear. "It's late," he rasped. "Go to sleep."

Turning on his heel, he headed for the study and a response from his New York team before he changed his mind and gave in to temptation.

He had a problem. A big one. Now he had to figure out what to do with it.

Chiara woke late, her body still adjusting to the time difference, her mind attempting to wrap itself around the intimate, late-night encounter she'd had with Lazzero the night before. She eyed the unruffled side of the bed opposite her, indicating Lazzero had not joined her. Which actually wasn't the worst thing that could have happened given how he'd walked away last night, shutting things down between them.

Her stomach knotted into a tight, hard ball. She kicked off the silk comforter in deference to the already formidable heat and stared moodily out at another vivid blue, cloudless perfect day through floor-to-ceiling windows bare of the blinds she'd forgotten to close. She might be able to excuse herself for her slip last night because she'd been so vulnerable in the moment, but she couldn't escape the emotional connection she and Lazzero had shared. How *amazing* he'd been.

She buried her teeth in her lip. She had poured her heart and soul out to him last night. Her hopes, her dreams. Instead of brushing them aside as her father had done, pointing to her mother who'd barely been eking out an income as a seamstress before she'd met him, or Antonio, who had advised her she'd be lost in a sea of competition, Lazzero had validated her aspirations.

Defeating the mean girls is your mission statement in life. If you quit—they win.

She'd never thought about it like that. Except now that she had, she couldn't stop. Which was unrealistic, she told herself as a distant, long-ago buried dream clawed itself back to life inside of her. Even with the bakery on a solid financial footing, the rent was astronomical. She'd still need to help her father out on the weekends because he couldn't afford the staff. Which would make studying and working impossible.

She buried the thought and the little twinge her heart gave along with it. It was easy to think fanciful thoughts in Lazzero's world, because he made everything *seem* possible. Everything *was* possible for him. But she was not him and this was not her world.

She conceded, however, that she had misjudged him that day in the café. Had tarred him with the same brush as Antonio, which had been a mistake. Antonio had been born with a silver spoon in his mouth, recklessly wielding his power and privilege, whereas Lazzero had made himself into one of the most powerful men in the world *despite* the significant traumas he'd suffered early on in life. He was a survivor. Just like her.

It made him, she acknowledged with dismay, even more attractive. It also explained so much about who he was, *why* he was the way he was, that insane drive of his. Because he would never be his father. Never see his world shattered beneath his feet again. It also, she surmised, explained why Lazzero was a part of the community angel organization in New York—it was his way of helping when he had been unable to help his father. Another piece of the man she was just beginning to understand.

Then there was last night. He could have used their intense sexual chemistry to persuade her into bed—but he had not. He had walked away instead. Exactly the opposite of what Antonio had done when he had seduced her with his champagne and promises.

Promises Lazzero would never give because he was clear about what he offered a woman. About what he had to give. Which would likely, she concluded, heat blanketing her insides, be the most incredible experience of her life if she allowed it to happen. Which would be *insane*.

She needed coffee. Desperately. She slipped on shorts and a T-shirt and ventured out to the kitchen to procure it. *All* problems could be solved with a good cup of java.

Making an espresso with the machine in the spotless, stainless steel masterpiece of a kitchen, she leaned against the counter and inhaled the dark Italian brew. She had nearly regained her equilibrium when Lazzero came storming into the kitchen dressed in jeans and a T-shirt, a dark cloud on his face. Sliding to an abrupt halt, he scorched his gaze over her fitted T-shirt and bare legs. Back up again.

"Make me one of those, will you?"

Heat snagged her insides. "You might try," she suggested with a lift of her chin, "'please make me one of your amazing espressos, Chiara. I am highly in need.'"

"Yes," he muttered, waving a hand at her. "All of that."

She turned and emptied the tamper into the garbage, relieved to escape all of that mouthwateringly disheveled masculinity. Took her time with the ritualistic packing of the grinds, because she had no idea where she and Lazzero stood after last night. How to navigate this, because it felt as if something fundamental had changed between them. Or maybe it was just *her* that felt that way?

Having artfully packed the tamper with the requisite perfect, round puck, she set the coffee to brew, turned around and leaned a hip against the counter. "You've been up all night?"

Lazzero raked a hand through his rumpled hair. "The designs are not what they need to be."

"When is your meeting with Gianni?"

"Tuesday."

She took a sip of her coffee. Considered his combustible demeanor from over the rim of her cup. "I have a thought."

He gave her a distracted look. "About what?"

Definitely past the moment, he was. "Volare," she elaborated. "I was looking at the Fiammata shoes when I was window-shopping yesterday. The way they are marketed. They're selling a dream with Volare, not a shoe. A *lifestyle*. The ability to fly no matter who you are. Your designs," she said, picking up one of the sheaf of drawings he'd left on the counter, "need to reflect that. They need to be aspirational."

He eyed her contemplatively. "You may have a point there. The designs are *functional*. That's what I don't like about them. Fiammata's approach is very European. Quality of life seems to predominate here. Which, in today's market," he allowed, "might appeal to the American consumer." He slanted her a speculative look. "What would you do with them?"

Chiara found her sketchpad in the bedroom and brought it back to the kitchen. Setting it on the island, she began sketching out a running shoe that was more aspirational than the one Lazzero's designers had done. Something she could see herself wearing.

"Something like this," she said, when she was finished. "Smoother lines. As if the shoe allows you to soar no matter who you are or what you do."

Lazzero rubbed a palm over the thick stubble on his jaw. "I like it, but I think we can go even further with it if that's the direction we were to take. Can you give it the sense that it has wings? My scientists can make sure the aerodynamics work. It's the impression that counts."

She altered the image so it looked even sleeker, with an emphasis on the power of the front of the shoe. Made the back end less clunky. "Like this?"

Lazzero studied it. "Now it's too aspirational. Too ethereal. It needs to be *real* at the same time it's inspirational."

She eyed him. "Are you always this perfectionistic?"

"Sì," he drawled, his gaze glimmering as it rested on

her. "With everything I do. It can be a good quality, I promise you."

Heat pooled beneath her skin, his well-satisfied comment slicing through her head. She wished he'd never said it because she couldn't get it out of her head.

She bent her head and fixed the drawing. Back and forth they went, building off each other's ideas, Lazzero relentlessly pushing her to do better, pulling things out of her she hadn't even known she had. Finally, they finished. She massaged her cramping hand as he examined the drawing from every angle. If he didn't like this version, she decided, he could do it himself.

"I love it," he said slowly, looking up at her. "You're insanely good, Chiara."

A glow warmed her insides. "It's rough."

"It's fantastic." He waved the drawing at her. "Do you mind if I get my New York team to play with the idea? See what they come up with?"

She shook her head. "Go ahead."

He prowled toward her. Dipped his head and grazed her cheek with his lips, the friction of his thick stubble against her skin, the intoxicating whiff of his expensive scent, unearthing a delicious firework of sensation in her. "Thank you."

She sank back against the counter, watching as he strode toward the living room.

"Oh, and, Chiara?"

Her pulse jumped in her throat as he turned around. "Mmm?"

A wicked smile curved his lips. "You make a mean espresso."

CHAPTER SEVEN

"SANTO CIELO."

Pia shaded her eyes from the bright sunlight slanting through the roof of San Siro stadium as the referee added two minutes to the Americas versus Western Europe game, the teams locked two-two in the tense, bitter rivalry being played in front of eighty thousand screaming fans. "I can't bear to watch," her Italian friend groaned. "Valentino is going to be *impossibile* if this ends in a tie."

Chiara, thankful for the one and only ally she had, kept her thoughts to herself. She knew how important this game was to Lazzero. Had witnessed how dedicated he was to the REACH charity he supported in Harlem that kept kids off the street and on the court, the cause he was playing for this week. More layers to the man she had so inaccurately assessed at the beginning of all of this.

Who, along with his penchant to care deeply for the things that mattered to him, had a seemingly inexhaustible appetite for social connection if it contributed to the bottom line. The foreign correspondents' dinner on Saturday, cocktails at the British embassy on Sunday, a dinner meeting with the largest clothing retailer in the world last night at a posh Italian restaurant where they'd consumed wine expensive enough to eat up her entire monthly budget.

Plenty of opportunity for Lazzero to put his hands on her in those supposedly solicitous touches that sent far too much electricity through her body and plenty of opportunity for her to like it far more than she should.

She sank her teeth into her lip as Lazzero took the ball on the sidelines. It had been all business all the time. Which was exactly as it should have been. What she'd signed up for. What she'd *asked* for. Why then, did she feel so barefoot? Because the way she felt when she was with Lazzero made her feel alive in a way she hadn't for a very, very long time? Because feeling *something* felt good?

Her palms damp, her heart pounding, she watched as Lazzero yelled instructions to his teammates, then threw the ball in. Off the Americas team went, roaring down the field. Three neat passes, the final one from Lazzero to Lucca, and the ball was in the net.

The crowd surged to its feet with a mighty roar, Chiara along with it. One last fruitless drive by the Western Europe team and the clock ran out, signaling victory for the Americas. Lazzero, looking utterly nonplussed by his assist in the winning goal, turned and trotted off the field where he and Lucca were enveloped in a melee of congratulations.

Pia groaned. "There goes my chance for romance tonight. You, on the other hand," she said, tugging on Chiara's arm, "must go down to the field. It's La Coppa Estiva tradition to give the winning players a kiss. The television cameras love it."

Oh, no. Chiara dug her heels in. She was *not* doing that. But as the other wives and girlfriends filed onto the field, she realized she had no choice. Getting reluctantly to her feet, she left her purse with Pia and made her way down the stairs.

Lazzero eyed her as she approached, an amused light dancing in his dark eyes. *Thump* went her heart as she took him in. Sweat darkening his T-shirt, his hair slicked back from his brow, his game face still on, he was spectacular.

She pulled to a halt in front of him. Balanced her hands

on his waist as she stood on tiptoe to brush a kiss against his cheek. "Congratulations," she murmured. "You played a fantastic game."

He caught her jaw in his fingers, the wicked glint in his eyes sending a skitter of foreboding through her. "I think," he drawled, "they're going to expect a bit more than that."

Spreading his big palm against her back, he bowed her in a delicate arch, caged her against the unyielding steel frame of his powerful body. Her breath caught in her throat as he bent his head and took her mouth in a pure, unadulterated seduction that weakened her knees.

Her arms wound around his neck out of the pure need to keep herself upright. But then, her fingers got all tangled up in his gorgeous thick hair, *she* got all tangled up in the dark, delicious taste of him and the way he incinerated her insides, and the *plink, plink* of the camera flashes faded to a distant distraction.

Dazed, disoriented, she rocked back on her heels when he ended it, the hand he had wrapped around her hip holding her steady. Light blinding her eyes, a chorus of wolf whistles and applause raining down around them, she struggled to find her equilibrium.

Lazzero swept his sexy, devastating mouth across her cheek to her ear. "It almost felt as if you meant that, *angelo mio*."

She was afraid she might have.

"Finally got your priorities straight." Lucca issued the jab as he waltzed past, his posse trailing behind him. "You look amazing, *querida*. As always."

Lazzero's face darkened. "I can still put my fist through your face, Sousa."

Lucca only looked amused as he headed to a television interview with Brazilian TV. Chiara looked up at Lazzero, her heartbeat slowing to a more normal rhythm. "How did your meeting with Gianni go?"

His combustible expression turned satisfied. "He loved the sketches. Due in large part, to you. He's invited us to a dinner party on Friday night to discuss the partnership further."

She smiled. "That's amazing. Congratulations."

He retrieved the towel he had slung over his shoulder and wiped the sweat from his brow. "I thought I'd take you out to say thank you. Celebrate."

"With the team, you mean?"

"No," he said casually, slinging the towel over his shoulder. "Just us. I figured you'd had enough socializing. And, I have a surprise for you."

A *surprise*? A break from the relentless socializing? She was most definitely on board.

A slither of excitement skittered up her spine. "What should I wear?"

He shrugged. "Something nice. Wear one of your own dresses if you like. We can just be ourselves tonight."

It was a directive Lazzero might have reconsidered as he and Chiara stood on the tarmac at Milano Linate Airport in the late afternoon sunshine, her light pink dress fluttering in the wind. Empire-waisted and fitted with flowing long sleeves that somehow still left her shoulders bare, it was designed with multiple layers of some gauzy type of silk that looked as if she was wearing a flimsy scarf instead of a dress.

Which only came to midthigh, mind you, exposing a sweep of bare leg that held him transfixed. He was having dreams about those legs and what they would feel like wrapped around him, and that dress wasn't helping. The image of what he would like to do with her wasn't fit for public consumption.

Chiara gave him a sideways look as she proceeded

him up the steps into the jet. "You told me to wear what I wanted."

"I did and you look great." He kept his description to the bare minimum. "The dress is fantastic."

Her mouth curved into a smile that would have lit a small metropolis. "I'm glad you think so. It's one of mine."

The impact of that smile hit him square in the chest. *He was screwed*, he conceded. So royally screwed. But then again, he'd known that the moment she'd told him her story. When she'd quietly revealed her plan to defeat the mean girls of the world. It explained everything about the sharp, spiky skin that encased her. The fierce need for independence. The brave face she put on for the world, because he'd been exactly the same.

The difference between him and Chiara was that he had taught himself not to care. Made himself impervious to the world, and she had not. Which *should* label her as off-limits to him. Instead, he had the reckless desire to peel back more of those layers. To find the Chiara that lay beneath.

They flew down to the boot of Italy to Puglia, known for its sun, sea and amazing views. Sitting in the heel of the boot, it was tranquil and unspoiled, largely untouched by the masses of tourists who flocked to the country.

"It's stunning," Chiara breathed as they landed in Salento, nestled in the clear waters of the Adriatic, its tall cliffs sculpted by the sea.

"A friend of mine has a place here." Lazzero helped her down the steps of the jet, afraid she would topple over in those high heels of hers, which also weren't helping his internal temperature gauge. "It's unbelievably beautiful."

Her dress whipped up in the wind as they walked across the tarmac. He slapped a hand against her thigh as a ground worker stopped to stare. "Can you please *control* this dress?"

Hot color singed her cheeks. "It's the wind. Had I known

we were *flying* to dinner, I would have chosen something else."

And that would have been so, so sad. He ruthlessly pulled his hormones under control as he guided her to the waiting car, allowing her to slide in first, then walked around the car to climb in the other side. The town of Polignano a Mare, perched atop a twenty-meter-high limestone cliff that looked out over the crystal-clear waters of the Adriatic, was only a short drive away.

Known for its cliff diving, jaw-dropping caves carved out of the limestone rock that rose from the sea, as well as its excellent food, it held a wealth of charm as the sunset bathed it in a fiery glow. Suggesting they leave the car behind and walk the rest of the way to their destination to enjoy the view, Lazzero caught Chiara's hand in his.

Her gaze dropped to where their fingers were interlaced. "We're not in public," she murmured. "You don't have to do that."

"Sheer force of habit," he countered blithely. "Don't be so prickly, Chiara. We're holding hands, not necking in the street."

Which brought with it a whole other series of images that involved him backing her into one of the quaint, cobblestoned side streets and taking exactly what he'd wanted from the very beginning. Not helpful when added to *the dress*.

She left her hand in his. Was silent as they walked through the whitewashed streets toward the sea, the lanes bursting with splashes of fluorescent color from the vibrant window boxes full of brightly hued blooms. Then it was him wondering about his presence of mind, because the whole thing felt right in a way he couldn't articulate. Had never experienced before.

The Grotta Nascondiglio Hotel, carved out of the magnificent limestone rocks, rose in front of them as they neared the seafront. Chiara gasped and pointed at something to their right. "Are *those* the cliff divers? Good heavens, look where they're diving from."

They were high—twenty meters above the ground, diving from one of the cliffs that flanked the harbor below. But Lazzero shrugged a shoulder as they moved closer to watch. "It's perfectly safe. The water is more than deep enough."

"I don't care how deep it is," Chiara breathed. "That's *crazy*. I would never do it. Would you?"

"I promised my friend who lives here I would do it next year with him."

Her eyes went wide. "No way."

A smile pulled at his lips. "Sometimes you just have to take the leap. Trust that wherever it takes you, you will come out the other side, better, *stronger* than you were before. Life is about the living, Chiara. Trusting your gut."

Chiara's brain was buzzing as Lazzero escorted her inside the gorgeous Grotta Nascondiglio Hotel. It might have been the challenge he had just laid down in front of her. Or it could simply have been how outrageously attractive he looked in sand-colored trousers and a white shirt that stretched across his muscular torso, emphasizing every rippling muscle to devastating effect.

He didn't need anything else to assert his dominance over the world, she concluded, knees a bit unsteady. Not even the glittering, understated Rolex that contrasted with his deeply tanned skin as he pressed a hand to her back and guided her inside the restaurant. The aura of power, *solidity*, about him was unmistakable, his core strength formed in a life that had been trial by fire.

The warm pressure of his palm against her back as they walked inside the massive, natural cave unearthed an excitement all of its own. It was sensory overload as she looked around her at the warmly lit room that opened onto a spectacular view of the Adriatic.

"Tell me we have a table overlooking the water," she said, "and I will die and go to heaven."

Lazzero's ebony eyes danced with humor. "We have a table overlooking the water. In fact, I think it's that one right there."

She followed his nod toward a candlelit table for two that sat at the mouth of the cave, the only one left unoccupied. The only thing separating it from a sheer, butterfly-inducing drop to the sea was the cast-iron fence that ran along the perimeter of the restaurant. Chiara's stomach tipped over with excitement. It was utterly heart-stopping.

The maître d' appeared and led them toward their table. She slipped into the seat Lazzero held out for her and accepted the menu the host handed her. Pushing her chair in, Lazzero took the seat opposite her.

"Not exactly a little hole in the wall in the East Village," she murmured, in an attempt to distract herself from the thumping of her heart.

A speculative glimmer lit his dark eyes. "Are you calling this a *date*, Chiara Ferrante?"

Her stomach missed its landing and crashed into her heart. "It was a joke."

His sensual mouth curved. "You can't even say it, can you? Are you going to run for the hills now that we've gotten that out of the way?"

"Are you?" she asked pointedly.

"No." He sat back in his chair, the wine list in hand. "I'm going to choose us a wine."

He did not ask her preference because, of course, that wasn't how a date with Lazzero went. His women felt feminine and cared for. And she found herself feeling exactly that as he took control and smoothly ordered a bottle of Barolo.

It was, she discovered, a heady feeling given she'd been the one doing the taking care of for as long as she could remember.

"So," Lazzero said, sitting back in his chair when their glasses were full. "Tell me about this urban line of yours. What kind of a vision do you have for it?"

She snagged her lip between her teeth. "You really want to know?"

"Yes. I do."

She told him about the portfolio of designs she'd been working on ever since she was a teenager. How her vision had been to design a line for both teenagers and young women starting out in the work force, neither of whom had much disposable income.

"Most women in New York can't afford designer fashion. Most are like me—they want to be able to express their individuality without blowing their grocery budget on a handbag."

Lazzero made a face. "I've never understood the whole handbag thing." He pointed his glass at her. "How would you market it, then?"

"Online. My own website, which would include a blog to drive traffic to the retail store. The boutique online fashion retailers... Keep it small and targeted."

"Smart," he agreed. "The trends are definitely headed that way. Very little overhead and no in-store marketing costs."

He swirled the rich red wine in his glass. Set his gaze on hers. "I was speaking with Bianca, my head designer, this morning when I signed off on the sketches. She mentioned to me how talented she thought you were."

Her insides warmed. "That's very nice of her to say."

"She's tough. It's no faint praise. Bianca," he elaborated, "heads up an incubator program in Manhattan, the

MFDA—Manhattan Fashion Designer Association. You've heard of it?"

She nodded. "Of course. They nurture new talent from the community—offer bursaries for school and co-op positions in the industry. It's an amazing mentoring program."

"I told Bianca your story. She wants to meet you." Lazzero's casually delivered statement popped her eyes wide-open. "If you are interested, of course. It would just be for a coffee. To see if you'd be a good fit for the group. There are no guarantees they'd take you on, but Bianca holds a great deal of sway."

Her stomach swooped and then dropped. "It's impossible to crack, Lazzero. Some of the most talented kids at school never made it in."

"They're looking for people with vision. You have one." He shook his head. "You don't second-guess an opportunity like this. You embrace it. See where it goes. It may go somewhere. It may go nowhere. But at least you tried."

She bit the inside of her mouth. She had only been dabbling at the drawing the past few years. What if she'd lost her technique? What if she didn't have *it* anymore? And then there was the part where she'd never get another chance like this.

"It's just a coffee," Lazzero said quietly. "Think about it."

She nodded. Sat back in her chair, her head spinning, and took a sip of her wine. The fact that he believed in her enough to do that for her ignited a glow inside of her. But it wasn't just that. He had invited her opinion about the sketches, had valued her input. He valued her for *who* she was. When was the last time someone had done that?

He might be every bit as much of a playboy as Antonio was, but that, she realized, was where the similarities between the two men began and ended. Lazzero was fascinating and complex, the depth to him undeniably compelling.

He was brutally honest about who he was and what he had to offer a woman, which Antonio had never been.

What he'd said that first night about her had been right. She *was* afraid to get hurt again. Was afraid to admit how she felt about him. But denying this connection between them wasn't getting her anywhere.

A flock of butterflies swooped through her stomach. What if she were to walk into this thing with Lazzero with her eyes wide-open? No wild, dreamy expectations like she'd had with Antonio. Just the cold hard reality that when she and Lazzero went back to New York, it would be over?

It was a heady thought that gained momentum as the conversation drifted from politics to the entertaining stories Lazzero had to tell about the mega-million-dollar athletes he worked with. As she sipped the delicious, full-bodied wine. Absorbed the heart-stoppingly romantic atmosphere as the waves crashed against the cliff below.

And then there was the way Lazzero kept holding her hand as if it was the most natural thing in the world. The brush of his long, muscular legs against the bare skin of her thighs that sent shivers of excitement through her. The way his gaze rested on her mouth with increasing frequency as the night wore on.

She didn't want to feel dead inside anymore. She wanted to walk into the fire with Lazzero. To know every thrilling moment of it. To not look back and wonder *what if.* Because she *wasn't* the same girl she'd once been. She was tougher. Wiser. And she knew what she wanted.

Somewhere along the way, between a discussion of the current state of the EU and the choice of decadent dessert, she lost the plot completely.

Lazzero's gaze darkened. "I have a question," he asked huskily, eyes on hers. "When are we getting to the necking part of the evening?"

Her insides fell apart on a low heated pull. "Lazzero—"

He lifted his hand. Signaled their waiter. Five minutes later, he had the bill paid and something else the waiter had placed in his hand. Extending a purposeful hand to her, he navigated the sea of tables to the exit with an impatience that had her heart slamming into her breastbone. But he didn't lead her toward the entrance, he directed her toward the elevators instead.

"Aren't we getting the car?" she breathed.

"No." Jamming his thumb on the call button Lazzero summoned the elevator. *A key*, she identified past her pounding heart. He had a key in his hand.

She could have cried out with frustration when the elevator doors opened to reveal two couples inside. She smiled politely at them, her knees shaking. Lazzero, noticing her less-than-steady stature, slid an arm around her waist and pulled her back against his hard, solid frame. Which was like touching dry timber to a match. By the time they stopped at their floor, she was trembling so much, she could hardly breathe.

Open slid the elevator doors. Out she and Lazzero stepped. Down the hall he strode, her hand in his. There didn't seem to be any other rooms on this floor, just the one door Lazzero stopped in front of at the end. Expecting him to use the key, she gasped as he backed her up against the wall instead, his mouth dipping to take hers in a hot, hard kiss, one that promised a wildness that echoed the shaking in her knees.

His hand wound around a thick chunk of her hair, he angled her head until he had her exactly where he wanted her, then plunged deeper, until they were consuming each other with a ferocity that was terrifying in its intensity.

When they finally came up for air, they were both breathing hard. Lazzero dragged his mouth up to her ear. "You are so beautiful," he murmured. "Tell me you want this, Chiara."

A moment of complete and utter panic consumed her. She drew back, a handful of his shirt in her fingers. Took a deep breath and grounded herself in his dark, hot gaze. In the man, she was learning, she could trust without reservation. Reaching up, she traced the hard, sensual line of his mouth with her fingers and nodded.

His eyes turned to flame. His brief fumble with the key before he got it into the lock wiped away the last of her reservations. Door unlocked, he picked her up, wrapped her legs around him and walked through the door, kicking it shut.

Wild for her in a way he had never experienced before, Lazzero backed Chiara up against the wall and picked the kiss up where he had left off. Trailing openmouthed caresses down the elegant line of her neck, he sank his teeth into the vein that throbbed for him. Her gasp rang out, hot, needy.

Tempted beyond bearing, he slid his hands beneath the gauzy silk of her dress and cupped her bottom. *Silk.* She was wearing silk panties beneath the dress—light, sheer wisps of nothing. Sliding his hands over her bottom, wanting, *needing* to feel her against him, he lifted her, altered the angle between them so that he was cradled in the heat between her thighs. She gasped as the still-covered length of his erection parted her softness through the silk of her panties.

"God, Lazzero. That feels—"

He smoothed a thumb over the juncture of her thigh and abdomen. She arched against him, his hot, hard length rubbing against her center.

"How?" he whispered, his voice rough. "How does it make you feel?"

"So good," she whimpered. "It feels so good. So *hot*."

He uttered a string of curses. *Slow it down*, his brain warned. Slow it down or he'd be buried in her in about five seconds flat and that was not how this was going to go. Not when the thought of having her was blowing a hole in his brain.

His heart threatening to batter its way through his chest, he sucked in a breath. Unwrapped her legs from around his waist and eased her down his body until her feet touched the floor, the slide of her curves against him hardening him to painful steel. Confused, Chiara stared up at him, her green eyes dazed with desire.

"We need to slow it down," he said huskily, snaring her hand and leading her into the suite, "or this is going to be over way too fast."

The suite, he discovered, was like something straight out of a fantasy. Carved out of the same limestone rock as the rest of the hotel, the circular room was finished with exposed brick and a mosaic-tiled floor illuminated by the soft glow of the lamp that had been left on for them.

Not to be outdone by the view from the restaurant, a luxurious sitting area offered a spectacular view of the sea through the open French doors and the terrace beyond. It was, however, the massive bed dominating the space that held his attention.

He sat down on it. Drew Chiara between his parted legs. His blood fizzled in his veins as he scoured her from head to toe.

"I don't know what to touch first," he admitted huskily. "You are so stunning you make my head want to explode."

Her eyes darkened to twin pools of forest green. She apparently knew exactly what *she* wanted to touch. Hands trembling, she moved her fingers to the buttons of his shirt. Worked her way down the row until she'd reached the last, buried beneath his belt. Dragging his shirt from his pants, she undid it, spread her palms flat against his abs and traced her fingers over each indentation and rise of muscle.

"You are insane," she murmured.

His stomach contracted, a rush of heat flooding through him. Not as insane as he was going to be if he didn't touch her soon. Shrugging off the shirt, he threw it to the floor. Hands at her waist, he turned her around and lowered the zip on her dress, exposing inches of creamy, olive skin as he sent the dress fluttering to the floor in a cloud of dusky-pink silk.

"Step out of it," he instructed, heart jamming in his chest.

She kicked the dress aside and turned around. Absorbed the heat of his gaze as it singed every inch of her skin. The soft, full, oh-so-kissable mouth that had driven him wild from the beginning. The delicate pink bra and panty set she wore that did little to hide the lush femininity beneath.

He sank his hands into her waist and lifted her to straddle him, her knees coming down on either side of his. Cupping her head with the palm of his hand, he brought her mouth down to his. Devoured her until she was soft and malleable beneath his hands and as into this as he was.

Needing to touch, to discover, he dropped his hands to her closure of her bra. Undid it and stripped it off, dropping it to the floor. Her curves, heavy and rose-tipped, filled his hands. Drunk on her, unable to get enough, he traced circles around her flesh with his thumbs, moving ever closer to the swollen tips with every sweep of his fingers, but never where she wanted it, until she groaned and pushed herself into his hands.

"Like this?" he asked softly, rubbing his thumbs over the distended peaks, enflamed by her response. She gasped and muttered her assent. He rolled the hard nubs between his fingers until she was twisting against him, restless and needy.

"You want more?" he murmured. "Show me where."

A wave of color stained her cheeks. "Lazzero—" she whispered.

"Show me."

She sank her teeth into her lip. Spread a palm against her abdomen, low, where those tiny pink panties barely covered her femininity. His blood surged in his veins. Tempted beyond bearing, he covered her palm with his, his eyes on hers. "You want me to touch you?"

Her cheeks turned a deeper, fiery red. Then came a tiny nod. He almost lost it right there, but somehow, he held it together. Easing his fingers beneath the waistband of her panties, he cupped her in his palm. Waited while she got used to his intimate possession, her beautiful green eyes dilating with heat. Then, sliding a finger along her slick cleft, he caressed her with a lazy stroke. Felt his heart slam in his chest at how wet, how aroused she was.

"You feel like honey," he murmured, taking her mouth in a lazy kiss at the same time as he rotated his thumb against her sweet, throbbing center. "Like hot, slick honey."

She moaned into his mouth. He kept teasing her until she was even hotter, slicker, aroused to a fever pitch. Then he slid a finger inside of her—slowly, gently, watching the pleasure flicker across her face as he claimed her with an intimate caress.

"You like that?"

"More," she whispered, arching her back.

Her uninhibited, innocent responses affected him like nothing he could remember, the blood raging in his head now. He slid deeper, each gentle push of his finger taking him further inside her silky body. The feel of her velvet flesh clenching around him was indescribable. She was tight and so damn hot. *Heaven.*

"That's it," he encouraged thickly as she moved into his touch, inviting it now. "Ride me, baby. Take your pleasure."

She closed her eyes. He tangled his tongue with hers, absorbed every broken sound until her harsh pants became desperate. "Lazzero—" she breathed.

He slid two fingers inside of her. Pumped them deep. Once, twice, three times, and she came apart in his arms.

Chiara wasn't sure how long it took her to surface, her bones melted into nothing as his strong arms held her upright. When she finally returned to consciousness, she found herself drowning in the dark glitter of satisfaction in his black gaze.

He had given her extreme pleasure, but had taken none for himself. The tense set of his big body beneath her hands was testament to the control he had exerted over himself. But now it was stretched to the limit.

Emboldened by what they'd just shared, wanting to give him the same pleasure he'd just given her, she dropped her hand to the hard ridge that strained his trousers. Reveled in the harsh intake of air he sucked in. "I think we should abstain from that right now," he murmured, clamping his hand over hers.

"I want to touch you," she said softly, her eyes on his. "Let me."

He considered her for a moment, and then his hands fell away. She curled her fingers around the button of his pants. Released it from its closure. Her fingers moving to his zipper, she lowered it, working it carefully past his straining erection.

The air was so hot and heavy between them as she reached inside his briefs and closed her fingers around him, it was hard to breathe. He was insanely masculine—like smooth, hard steel. Moving her hands over him, she stroked him, petted him, her body going slick all over again at the thought of having him. *Taking* him.

With a low groan, Lazzero rolled off the bed and divested himself of the rest of his clothes. The sound of a foil wrapper sounded inordinately loud in the whisper-quiet room. Prowling back to the bed, he kissed her again, eased her back into the soft sheets with the weight of his body and stripped the panties from her.

An ache building inside of her in a deeper, headier place, she cupped the back of his head and brought his mouth down to hers.

Luxurious, intimate, the meeting of their mouths went on forever. Sliding his hand around the back of her knee, Lazzero curved her leg around his waist. Settled himself into the cradle of her thighs until his heat was positioned against her slick, wet flesh. Her stomach dissolved into dust. He was big. *So big.*

"We go slow," he murmured, reading her expression. "Tell me how it feels, *caro*. What you like."

She arched her hips, desperate for him. He slid a palm beneath her bottom, raised her up and slipped the velvet head of him just inside her, his big body shuddering. "So tight," he said raggedly, "so good. How does that feel?"

"Amazing." She barely got the word out past the pounding of her heart. "More."

He sank inside of her a little bit more. Retreated, then pushed deeper, each stroke giving her time to adjust to the size and girth of him. Gentle, so patient, he tried *her* patience.

She closed her hands around his rock-hard glutes and pulled him deeper. A muttered curse leaving his mouth, he grasped her hips and claimed her with a single, powerful thrust that filled every part of her. Tore the breath from her lungs.

Never had she felt so possessed, so full of *everything*. Mouth glued to his, her air his air, they set a frantic rhythm together until they melted into one. Until she felt herself tighten around him, the pleasure threatening to shatter her all over again.

"That's it." Thick, hoarse, the guttural edge to Lazzero's voice at her ear spurred her on. "Let go."

His big body flexed above her, his muscles bunching as he shifted his position to deepen his thrusts. The connection they shared as his dark gaze burned into hers was so electric, so all-encompassing, it froze her in place. So much more than just the physical, it was the most intimate, soul-baring experience of her life.

Slowly, deliberately, he ground against her where she needed him the most. The delicious friction of his body against hers sent her over the edge with a sharp cry. An animal-like groan leaving his throat, Lazzero unleashed himself and took his pleasure, claiming her so deeply all she saw was white-hot stars as they shattered into one.

CHAPTER EIGHT

CHIARA EMERGED FROM a sex-induced haze to find herself
plastered across Lazzero's muscular chest, her legs tangled
with his, his heart pounding beneath her ear in almost as
wild a rhythm as hers. She had the feeling he was as thrown
off balance by what they'd just shared as she was, but he
didn't say anything, just stroked a lazy path down her spine
with his palm.

Her stomach dipped, settling somewhere around the
rocky shore below. She'd just had wild, ridiculously hot
sex with Lazzero, the depth of the connection they'd shared
frightening in its intensity. She had not only walked *into*
the fire, she'd drowned herself in it. She didn't feel dead
anymore, she felt unnervingly, terrifyingly alive, like someone had mainlined adrenaline through her veins. As if she'd
denied herself this depth of feeling, of *connection*, for so
long, it was complete and utter sensory overload.

But there was also fear. Fear she'd spent a lifetime avoiding these feelings. That the one time she'd slipped and allowed herself to be this vulnerable, she'd been destroyed.
Fear that it was Lazzero that was making it so scary. Because he was an insane lover. Because she had liked him
for a long time and refused to admit it.

Because of how he made her *feel*.

She buried her teeth in her lip. Forced herself to stay in
the moment. To absorb it, rather than run from it, because

she'd been doing that for far too long and she'd promised herself *this* was not going to be about that. This was about finding a piece of herself again that she'd lost.

"What?" Lazzero's hand stilled on her spine, as if he could read the shift in her emotion.

She buried her teeth deeper into her lip. "Nothing."

He rolled her onto her back and sank his fingers into her hair so that she was forced to look at him. "You are far too easy to read. You have smoke coming out of your ears. Regrets already?"

"No. It was perfect. I—" She shook her head. "Making myself vulnerable isn't the easiest thing for me. You were right about that. It's easier to hide behind my layers—to not engage, rather than let myself feel."

His midnight gaze warmed. "You were engaged just now. You made me a little insane for you, Chiara. Or did you miss the part where we almost didn't make it to the bed?"

A flush crept up her body and warmed her cheeks. She had *not* missed that part. She had been there for every mind-blowing second of it. She'd *liked* that he'd almost lost control. That she could do that to him. That he had been just as crazy for her as she had been for him. It made her feel less self-conscious about the way she felt.

Lazzero ran a finger across the heated surface of her cheek. "Give me five minutes," he murmured, "and I will refresh your memory."

Her gaze slipped away from his, unable to handle the intensity of the moment. Moved over the magnificent length of his muscled body, bathed in the glow of the lamplight. It warmed another part of her entirely, every inch of the honed, sinewy muscle on display, the scar that crisscrossed his knee his only imperfection.

She traced her fingers over the raised ridge of the scar. "What's this?"

"An old basketball injury."

"The one that ended your career?"

"Yes."

When no further information was forthcoming, she sank back on her elbow to look at him. "I sat beside your old basketball coach at lunch yesterday—Hank Peterson. He was wonderful. Full of such great stories. He told me you come to talk to his kids at the REACH program."

A ghost of a smile touched his mouth. "Hank is a legend. I met him when we moved to Greenwich Village. He used to coach a league at The Cage, one of the most famous streetball courts in New York that was right around the corner from our house. It was mythical, where *dreams* are made—where some of the greats were born. I used to ditch my homework and play all night. Until they turned the lights off and Hank sent me home."

Her mouth curved. "I used to do the same thing with my sketching. I was supposed to be doing my homework while my parents finished work at the bakery. Instead, my mother would come home to a whole lot of drawings in the back of my notebook and very little else. It used to drive her crazy."

"At least she cared," he murmured. "That's a good thing."

She frowned. "Yours didn't?"

"There was no one home *to* care. My father was drinking by then and my mother had left. Nico," he allowed, "used to lecture me to study. He was all about school and learning. But I was hopelessly obsessed."

Her eyes widened. *His mother had left?* "I thought she remarried when your father died."

Lazzero shook his head. "She walked out on us when I was fourteen."

Chiara was shocked into silence. *What mother would leave her children like that? When everything was falling*

apart around them? When her children were at their most
vulnerable and needed her most of all?

"Was your father's alcoholism an instigator in her leaving?" she asked, trying to understand.

"My mother was a sycophant," he said flatly. "She fell in love with my father's money and she fell out of love with him when he lost it."

She bit the inside of her mouth. "I'm sure it wasn't quite that simple."

"It was just that simple." He tucked his hands behind his head, an expressionless look on his face. "My mother was a dancer trying to make it on Broadway when she and my father met. She wanted a career, the glitz, the glamour. She didn't want a family. When she got pregnant with Nico, my father thought he could change her mind. But he never did. He spent their entire marriage trying to keep her happy, which in the end failed miserably when he imploded and she walked out on him."

She absorbed his harshly issued words. "That's only one side of the story," she said huskily. "I'm sure it couldn't have been easy on your mother to give up her career. Her *dream*. And your father," she pointed out, "sounds as if he was extremely driven. As if he had his own internal demons to battle. Which couldn't have been easy to live with."

"No," Lazzero agreed evenly, "it wasn't. But he was a man. He was focused on providing. He was hurt when he couldn't make her happy. His pride was damaged. He spent more and more time at work, because he didn't want to be at home, which eventually devolved into the affairs he had to compensate. Which were not in any way excusable," he qualified, "but perhaps understandable, given she drove him to it."

That struck a raw note given what Antonio had done to her. "Nobody drives anyone to do anything," she refuted.

"Relationships are complicated things, Lazzero. You make a choice to love someone. To see it through."

His eyes glittered. "Exactly why I choose not to do it. Because any way you look at it, someone always messes it up."

She absorbed his intense cynicism. "So basketball," she murmured, seeking to dispel some of the tension in the air, "became your outlet. Like sketching was for me?"

He nodded, sifting his fingers through her hair and watching it in the play of the light. "If I was on the court, I wasn't dealing with the mess my life was. With the shadow of a man my father had become. But I also," he conceded, his gaze darkening, "fell in love. There's a magic about the game when you play it on the streets of New York—an unspoken devotion to the game we all shared. By the time I'd won my first tournament for Hank, I knew I wanted to play basketball for a living."

Her mouth curved. "Hank said you were always the first and last on the court."

"Because I wasn't as physically gifted as some of the other players," he acknowledged. "I didn't have the size some of them did, nor the jumping ability. I had to work harder, *want it more* than all the rest. But I was smart. I could read the court and I built my career around that. I won a division championship for Hank in my junior year at Columbia."

A college career which, according to Hank, had been limitless in its possibilities. Until he'd injured himself.

She curled her fingers around his knee. "Tell me about it? What happened?"

He lifted a shoulder. "There isn't much to tell. I was chasing a player down on a breakaway in a key divisional play-off game. I jumped to block the shot, felt something pop in my knee. Shatter. When I tried to stand up, I couldn't. I'd torn the two main ligaments that hold your knee together. It was almost impossible for the surgeons to put it back together."

Her throat felt like gravel. "That must have been devastating."

"It was what it was."

His standard line. But she knew now it hadn't been so simple. "Hank said you were an exceptional player, Lazzero. That you'd been scouted by three professional teams. It had to have hurt to have that taken from you."

A shadow whispered over the clarity of his gaze. "What do you want me to say, Chiara? That I was shattered inside? That watching every dream I'd had since I was eight go up in a puff of smoke tore me apart?"

She flinched at the harsh edge to his voice. Pushed a hand into the mattress to sit up and stare out at the sea, a dark, silent mass beyond the French doors. Maybe she'd been looking for the truth, given she'd poured her heart and soul out to him on the terrace that night. But that was not what this was, she reminded herself, and she'd be a fool to forget it.

Lazzero exhaled an audible breath. Snared an arm around her waist and pulled her back against him, tucking her against his chest.

"I was in denial," he said quietly. "I refused to believe it would end my career. I went for a second opinion and when that doctor told me I would never play at that level again, I set out to prove him wrong. It took me almost a year and hundreds of hours of physio to accept the fact that I was never coming back. That it was *over*."

A hand fisted her chest. "You didn't give up," she said, absorbing the hard beat of his heart beneath her ear. "Not like I did."

"Giving up wasn't an option. It was everything to me."

Sometimes dreams are too expensive to keep.

Her blood ran jagged in her veins. Suddenly, he made so

much sense to her. Lazzero's world had dissolved beneath his feet, not once, when his father had imploded and his mother had walked out, but twice, when his basketball career had disintegrated beneath his feet on a painful stroke of fate. But instead of allowing himself to become bitter and disillusioned, he'd created Supersonic. Built a company around the sport he loved.

"Hank says you are a great mentor to the kids," she said huskily.

A lift of his shoulder beneath her. "It gives them something to shoot for if a pro basketball career doesn't work out for them. Unfortunately, the statistics are stacked against it."

Her heart did a funny twist. She hadn't needed another reason to like him this much. Because falling for Lazzero wasn't on the agenda in this walk on the wild side of hers. And maybe he decided that too, because before she could take another breath, he had rolled her onto her back, speared a hand into her hair, and there was no escaping the sparks that sizzled and popped between them.

"I think that's enough talking," he murmured, lowering his mouth to hers. "Now that I've gotten you where I want you, I intend to take full advantage of it."

She sucked in a breath, only to lose it as he covered her mouth with his, his kiss dragging her back into the inferno with relentless precision. A gasp left her throat as he slid his tongue inside her mouth, mating with her own in a fiery dance that signaled his carnal ambitions.

It was pure, dominant male at its most blatant and she loved it. Her hands found the thick muscle of his back and shoulders as she surrendered to the hunger that consumed them both.

Her last coherent thought was that it had been worth every second. Exactly as she'd known it would be. And maybe she was in way, way over her head.

* * *

An opera at the stunning Teatro alla Scala in Milan was hardly the thing to put a girl firmly back on her feet after she'd just embarked on a wild, passionate affair with a man who was most definitely out of her league. Chiara, however, attempted to do exactly that the following evening as she and Lazzero attended a private performance of Verdi's *La Traviata* at the beautiful, iconic theater.

An opportunity for the sponsors of La Coppa Estiva to entertain their international guests in a glamorous, glitzy affair that had been enjoyed by the Milanese upper crust since the eighteenth century, she and Lazzero were to host a German retail scion and his wife in their private box.

She thought Micaela had gotten her outfit just right, the ankle-length sleek scarlet dress with its asymmetric cut at the shoulder glamorous, yet understated, a red lip and sparkly heels her only accessories. It was Lazzero in a perfectly tailored black suit, his ebony hair worn fashionably spiky tonight, a five o'clock shadow darkening his jaw, that was making her pulse race.

His touch lingered just a little bit longer than before, the possessive glimmer in his eyes as they worked the crowd doing something funny to her insides. *As if they were lovers*. Which, in fact, they were, a mind-boggling detail she was just beginning to wrap her head around.

Then it was the spectacular theater that was stealing her attention. Six rows of gold stuccoed boxes sat stacked on top of each other in the oval theater, soaring high above the packed crowd below. The massive, Bohemian crystal chandelier was incredible, as was the sumptuous elegance of their box with its red velvet, silk and gilded stucco interior. Since she knew nothing about opera, having never attended one in her life, Chiara nestled her viewing glasses in her lap and scoured the program so she would know the story, but soon the lights were dimming and the curtain came up and she lost herself to the performance instead.

She was hooked from the very first second. Transfixed by the elaborate sets, the hauntingly beautiful music and the poignant story of Violetta Valéry, the heroine of Verdi's opera.

Violetta, a courtesan, knows she will die soon, exhausted by her restless life. Alfredo Germont, played by a handsome, world-famous tenor who strutted across the stage in the opening act, has been fascinated by Violetta for a very long time. When he is introduced to her at a party, he proposes a toast to true love. Enchanted by his candid and forthright manner, Violetta responds with a toast in praise of *free* love.

Enamoured though she may be, Violetta decides there is no room for such emotion in her life and walks away from Alfredo. But she can't quite seem to put him out of her head and eventually, the two embark on a passionate love affair.

Tears filled Chiara's eyes as she watched Alfredo awaken Violetta's desire to be truly loved. They slipped silently down her cheeks amidst the beautiful music. She brushed them from her cheeks, afraid to watch, because she knew what was to come. As in all of the great, tragic love stories it seemed, disaster was about to befall the two lovers.

Alfredo's father, a wealthy aristocrat, pays a visit to Violetta to convince her there can be no future for her and his son. That she is destroying Alfredo's future by encouraging his love, and that of his sister, as well, to marry into the upper echelons of society.

Heartbroken, Chiara watched as Violetta left Alfredo to return to her old life, telling him she didn't love him to set him free. Alfredo, grief stricken and racked with jealousy and hurt at Violetta's supposed betrayal, stalked across the stage as the music reached its crescendo and proposed a duel with her paramour to end the second act.

"Ooh," said the German CEO's wife as the lights came up for the intermission. "It's so good, isn't it?"

Chiara nodded, frantically rifling through her purse for a tissue. Lazzero offered her the handkerchief from his front pocket, a cynical look on his face. She ignored him as they made their way out into the elegant foyer with its fluted columns and crystal chandeliers, her head still caught up in the story. Absorbing its nuances.

Violetta's story had struck so many chords in her, she wasn't sure which one to consider first. How much the character reminded her of herself with her determination to escape her emotions. How she hadn't been good enough for Antonio. How swept up she was becoming in Lazzero. What would happen in the end, because Violetta had to die, didn't she? Would her and Alfredo's love be forever thwarted?

When her opera companion excused herself to the ladies' room, Chiara slipped out onto one of the Juliette balconies to regain her equilibrium while Lazzero introduced the German CEO around. The tiny balcony, set apart from the larger one that was buzzing with activity, boasted a lovely view of the lit Piazza della Scala.

She leaned back against the stone facade of the building and inhaled a deep breath of the sultry, summer night air. It was as far removed from her life as she could possible imagine. And yet, there was something so real about the moment. So revelatory.

She had not been living for far too long, that she knew. But was it worth the consequences that Violetta had feared to fully embrace this new world of emotion? To reap the greatest rewards that life had to offer? She hadn't quite determined the answer to that question when Lazzero stepped out onto the balcony, two glasses of Prosecco in his hands.

She lifted a brow. "You're not networking until you drop?"

"Hans saw someone he knew." He handed her a glass of Prosecco. "I thought you might need this. You looked a little emotionally devastated in there."

A wry smile pulled at her mouth. "It's a beautiful story. I got a little swept up in the emotion. Although you," she conceded, "did not seem quite so captivated. Which part of your jaded view of love did Verdi offend?"

"Not all of it," he drawled, leaning a hip against the wall. "I thought Violetta was spot-on. I'm all for the concept of *free love*. Everybody walks into it with realistic expectations. Nobody gets hurt. Her critical mistake was in buying into Alfredo's vision—into a fantasy that doesn't really exist."

"Who says?" she countered lightly. "My parents had it. They were madly in love with each other."

"So much so that your father is in the dark place that he is?" Lazzero tipped his head to the side. "Some would call that an unhealthy kind of love. A *devastating* kind of love."

She couldn't necessarily disagree with the observation, because loving that deeply had consequences. She had lived with them since she was fifteen. She knew what it was like to be loved and what it felt like to have that love taken away. Had convinced herself she was better off without it after Antonio. But she also believed her parents had shared something special and somewhere, deep down, if she were to be completely honest, she knew she wanted it too.

She met Lazzero's cynical gaze. "You're talking about your parents. That *messy*, kind of love you are so intent on avoiding?"

"They were a disaster from start to finish," he said flatly. "My father fell in love with an illusion rather than the reality of what he got. This," he said, waving a hand toward the doors, "could be their story tonight. And you see how well it turned out for Violetta and Alfredo."

She shook her head. "Violetta *loved* Alfredo. What they had was real. It was his father that messed it up."

"And look how easily she was swayed. One might say she was simply looking for a way out. That she never truly committed."

"She was being selfless. She wanted to set him free. You make a choice to love someone, Lazzero. You *choose* to commit."

"Or you choose to marry for the wrong reasons." He tipped his glass at her. "My mother married my father for the money. Carolina married Gianni on the rebound. Violetta needed to be rescued. Does anyone ever marry for the *right* reason? Because they want to spend their lives together?"

"Violetta's case was different," she disagreed. "For her to set Alfredo free was, in my opinion, the ultimate act of love on her part."

"And what happens when she is gone?" Lazzero lifted a dark brow. "Do you think Alfredo is going to applaud himself for the decision he made when his heart has been smashed to smithereens?"

Exactly as his father's had been? Her insides curled at the parallels. "Maybe," she offered huskily, "he will feel lucky to have experienced that kind of love *once* in his life and he will have that to hang on to when she's gone. Maybe, as much pain as my father is in, he wouldn't trade what he and my mother had for the world."

Lazzero rested an inscrutable gaze on her.

"What?"

"You," he murmured. "I never would have guessed you are a closet romantic with that prickly exterior of yours."

She shrugged. "I'm merely trying to make a point. *You* are the one who said to me that tarring all men of a certain bank balance with the same brush is a mistake. Maybe," she suggested, "lumping all relationships into the same category is an equal error in judgment."

He pushed away from the wall and caged her in with a palm beside her head all in one lazy movement. "So," he drawled, his eyes on hers, "is that what is on offer to Mr. Right? Chiara Ferrante's heart if a man is willing to go *all in*?"

Her breath stalled in her chest. He was so gorgeous, so dark and brooding up close, it was impossible to think. "Stop playing with me," she murmured. "You are inherently skilled in the art of deflection, Lazzero."

"Who says I'm playing? Maybe I'm accepting your challenge. Maybe I just want to know the answer."

"Maybe," she breathed. Because she wasn't sure if she was ready to open herself up again to the full gamut of that emotion she so feared. To the possibility she might be rejected again—that she wouldn't be *good enough*. But maybe that was the risk you had to take. To know, that if you jumped, you were strong enough to handle whatever came on the other side.

"What I *think*," Lazzero murmured, his dark gaze glittering as it rested on hers, "is that you and I have a good thing, Chiara. Honest, up-front, with all of our cards on the table. And *that* is why it works."

Right, she told herself. That was exactly what this was. And she could handle it. Absolutely she could.

"Although," he said softly, lowering his head to hers so their breaths melded in a warm, seductive caress, "I didn't come out here to debate Verdi with you."

Every kiss, every caress, every heart-stopping moment of pleasure from the night before swept through her in a heady rush. "Oh," she breathed, her heart thumping in her chest. "Why did you?"

"Because I wanted to do *this*." He closed his mouth over hers in a lazy, persuasive possession that stormed her senses. She let her eyes flutter shut. Stopped thinking entirely as her fingers curled around the lapel of his jacket, a gasp of warm air leaving her lips as her mouth parted beneath his sensual assault.

The sound of the intermission bell ended the seductive spiral. "We should go back in," Lazzero murmured, nuzzling her mouth.

"Yes," she agreed unsteadily, taking a step back. "Although I'm not so sure I want to see Violetta shatter Alfredo's heart."

CHAPTER NINE

THE THOUGHT OF a dinner party at Villa Alighieri, Gianni
Casale's stunning estate in Lake Como, was a much less
intimidating prospect for Chiara than many of the events
she and Lazzero had attended thus far. She had created the
sketches for Volare the Italian CEO had fallen in love with,
she had accepted Bianca's offer for coffee which could take
her life in a whole new direction and she was knee-deep
in a spectacular affair with Lazzero that showed no signs
of cooling.

If she was being unwise, foolhardy, in thinking she could
handle all of this, telling herself she wasn't in as deep as
she was, she brushed those thoughts aside, because being
with Lazzero was the most breathtakingly exciting experience of her life, she felt ridiculously alive and it was the
headiest of drugs.

Striving for an elegance and composure to match the
evening, she chose a midlength, black wrap dress. Simple
in design, it was the gorgeous material that made the dress,
the light jersey clinging to her body in all the right places,
the deeply cut V that revealed the barest hint of the swell
of her breasts its only overtly sexy note.

Chiara had loved it because of the huge, red hibiscus
that fanned out from her waist, transforming the dress from
ordinary to extraordinary. A splash of vibrant color on a
perfectly cut canvas.

Adding a dark cherry gloss to her lips and delicate high heels that matched the exotic bloom, she left the golden tan she'd acquired to do the rest of the work, her final touch a series of layered silver bracelets.

Lazzero spent the entire drive up to Lake Como on a conference call, in full mogul mode. It wasn't until they'd parked at the marina and taken possession of the boat that would transport them to Villa Alighieri, that she claimed his attention, his gaze roving over her in a starkly appreciative appraisal that brought a flush to her cheeks.

"You look like an exotic flower come to life," he murmured, brushing a kiss against her cheek. She took in his tapered, light gray pants and lavender shirt as he stepped back. They did everything for his dark good looks and little for her pounding heart that felt as if it might push right through her chest.

On any other man, the pastel color might have come off as less than masculine. On Lazzero, it was a look that would send most women slithering to the ground.

"You don't look so bad yourself," she said breezily, the understatement of the year. But clearly, she needed to do something to diminish the way his eyes on her made her feel. As if this was more than a charade. As if she wanted to fling caution to the wind. Which was so *not* what she should be doing.

His dark gaze trailed lazily over her face. Read the emotions coursing through her as he always seemed to do. "I am," he drawled, "worried about the hair, however."

She produced a scarf from her evening bag. "I was warned." Draping it around her head, she secured the ends beneath her chin in Jackie O fashion before Lazzero handed her into the boat and brought the powerful speedboat rumbling to life. Soon, they were off, headed toward Villa Alighieri, which was perched at the end of a wooded promontory on the far end of the lake, accessible only by boat because the privacy-conscious Gianni liked it that way.

The sun threw up slender fingers of fire into a spectacular vermillion sky, the air was crisp and cool on her skin, the spray of the seawater as they sped across the lake salty, invigorating, life affirming in a way she couldn't describe. Or maybe, she thought, butterflies swooping through her stomach, that was just the way Lazzero made her feel—as if she'd woken up from a life of not really living.

When a particularly strong gust of wind caught her off guard, she swayed in her high heels. Lazzero caught her wrist in his fingers, tugged her to him and tucked her in front of him at the steering wheel. His mouth at her ear, he pointed out the sights, the husky edge to his voice raking across her nerve receptors, backed up by the hard press of his amazing thighs against hers. By the time he cut the throttle and they pulled up to the wide set of stone steps that led up to Villa Alighieri, Chiara was so caught up in him she couldn't see straight.

Lazzero threw the rope to one of the valets who stood waiting, then lifted her out of the boat and onto the steps, his hands remaining on her waist to steady her as her legs adjusted to solid ground. Drawn by the smoky heat in his eyes, she stared up at him, the muscles in her throat convulsing.

"Dammit, Chiara." He raked a gaze over her face. "You pick a hell of a time to go there, you know that?"

You don't pick *these things*, she thought unsteadily, sliding her hand into his as he led her up the path toward the cream stuccoed villa, which rose up out of the spectacular, terraced gardens.

"This is unbelievable," she murmured. *"Heaven."*

"Gianni named it after his favorite poet—Dante Alighieri—who wrote *The Divine Comedy.*"

Her lips curved. "My father loves *The Divine Comedy.*"

He'd been trying to get her to read it for forever. She thought it appealed to the philosopher in him.

He was quiet as they took the winding path through the gardens up to the loggia. But she knew how critical tonight was for him. Read it in the tense set of his face. Which meant she needed to be focused on the task at hand.

"Who's going to be here tonight?"

He threw her an absentminded look. "A few of the Italian players and their wives. A fairly intimate group from what I could gather."

Which it turned out to be. Mingling under the elegant loggia which offered a breathtaking view of the lake and the islands beyond from its perch on the highest point of the promontory, were perhaps a dozen guests.

Carolina and Gianni materialized to greet them. Lazzero slid a proprietary hand around her waist, but Carolina, it seemed, had elected to sheath her claws tonight. Which made it easier for Chiara to let down her guard as she met the Italian players and their wives and girlfriends, as well as Gianni's daughter from his first marriage, Amalia, a beautiful, sophisticated blonde.

The friendly rivalry between Lazzero and the Italian players inspired good-natured jokes and predictions about who would win the tournament, headed for an Americas, Western Europe collision in the final the following day. By the time they'd finished the cocktails, Chiara was relaxed and enjoying herself, finding Amalia, in particular, excellent company.

It was as they were about to sit down to dinner at the elegantly set table for twelve that Amalia's beautiful face lit up. *"Eccoti!"* she exclaimed, walking toward the house. *There you are.* "I thought maybe you were grounded by the bad weather."

Amalia's husband, Chiara assumed, who'd been in London on a business trip. She turned to greet him, a smile on her face. Felt her heart stop in her chest at the sight of the tall, dark-haired male brushing a kiss against Amalia's cheek, the jacket of his sand-colored suit tossed across his shoulder.

It could *not* be. *Not here. Not tonight.*

Amalia came back, her husband's hand caught in hers. "Antonio," she said happily, "please to meet you Lazzero Di Fiore, a member of the Americas team and a business associate of my father's, and his fiancée, Chiara Ferrante."

"Please *meet*." Antonio corrected her English, but his eyes never left Chiara. "*Mi dispiace.* I'm sorry I'm late. We were grounded for an hour."

"You're not late," Amalia said, wilting slightly at the correction. "We were just about to sit down to dinner."

"*Bene.*" Antonio held out a hand to Lazzero. "A pleasure," he drawled in perfectly accented English. "Congratulations on your engagement."

Chiara swayed on her feet. Lazzero tightened his arm around her waist, glancing down at her, but her eyes were glued to the man in front of her. His raven-dark hair, the lantern jaw she'd once loved, the piercing blue eyes that exuded an unmistakable power, an authority that was echoed in every line of his perfectly pressed, handcrafted suit. But it was his eyes that claimed her attention. They were the coldest she'd ever encountered.

How, she wondered, *had she never noticed that?*

Lazzero extended his hand to Antonio. Greeted the man who had once been her lover. Who had smashed her heart into so many pieces she'd wondered if she would ever be able to put herself back together again.

Panic pushed a hundred different flight routes through her head. What was she supposed to do? Admit she knew him? Deny it completely? The latter seemed preferable with his wife standing at his side. Antonio, however, didn't miss a beat. Focusing that cold, blue gaze on her, he bent to press a kiss to both of her cheeks. "Lazzero is clearly a lucky man," he murmured. "When is the big day?"

It was as if he'd asked her the exact date and time a meteor was going to hit the earth and blow them all to smithereens. Lazzero gave her a quizzical look. She swallowed hard and gathered her wits. "Next summer," she murmured. "So many people rush their engagements. We wanted to enjoy it."

"Indeed," agreed Antonio smoothly. "Marriage is a lifelong commitment. A serious endeavor. Amalia and I did the same."

Oh, my God. A flare of fury lanced through her. He had not just said that. *A lifelong commitment. A serious endeavor. He* had been willing to break those vows before he'd even embarked on his marriage. He had *planned* on taking a mistress, without deigning to fill her in on the plan. And why? Amalia was beautiful, charming, funny, *with* the impeccable breeding Antonio required.

Gianni joined them, giving Antonio's arm a congenial squeeze. "A good introduction for you," he said to Lazzero. "The Fabrizio family is the largest stakeholder in Fiammata outside of the family. That's how Antonio and Amalia met. You should pick his brain over dinner. He can give you some excellent perspective on the company."

Lazzero nodded and said he would do exactly that. Chiara attempted to absorb the panic seeping through her like smoke infiltrating a burning building. Of course it made complete sense that Antonio owned a stake in Fiammata, she acknowledged numbly. He ran one of Europe's largest investment houses, with a slew of marquee clients across the globe.

Lazzero bent his head to hers as they waited to be seated at the elegant table under the loggia, his lips brushing her cheek in a featherlight caress. "What's wrong?"

"Nothing." She forced a smile past her pounding heart. "I think that cocktail might have gone to my head."

"You should watch the wine, then. It was a hot day."

She absorbed the concern in his ebony gaze. The *warmth*. It was like looking into a mirror of the man. She always knew exactly where she stood with Lazzero—good or bad—just as he'd promised from the beginning.

She did not turn down the excellent Pinot Grigio that was served with the appetizer, desperately needing the steadying edge it gave her nerves. Seated between Amalia and Lazzero, with Antonio directly opposite her and Gianni beside him, she attempted to regain her composure as the men talked business and Amalia chattered on. But it was almost impossible to concentrate.

Antonio kept staring at her, making only a cursory attempt at conversation. Which made her agitated and furious all at the same time. She took a deep sip of her wine. Steeled herself as she pulled her gaze away from his. She was going to do exactly what she'd told herself she would do in this situation. She was going to move past it like the piece of history it was. She was not going to let Antonio get to her and she was not going to let her disarray affect this evening for Lazzero.

Somehow, she made it through the leisurely seven-course meal that seemed to stretch for an eternity on a hot, sultry night in the Lakes, the wine flowing as freely as the delicious food, which Chiara could only manage a few bites of. By the time the *dolce* was served, and Gianni claimed Lazzero for a private conversation over a *digestivo* of grappa, she was ready to crawl out of her skin.

She chatted fashion with Amalia, who was quite the fashionista with the budget she had at her disposal. When Carolina claimed Amalia to speak with someone else, Chiara secured directions to the powder room at the bottom of the loggia stairs and retreated to repair her powder and gloss. A tension headache pounding like the stamp of a sewing machine in her head, she took her time, aware Gianni and Lazzero might be a while and unable to face the thought of yet more social chitchat.

When she could delay no longer, she headed back upstairs. Almost jumped out of her skin when Antonio cut her off at the bottom of the stairs.

"We need to talk," he said grimly.

A thread of unease tightened around her chest, then unraveled so fast her heart began to whirl. "No we don't. We were done the day I walked out of your penthouse. There's nothing to talk about."

He set his piercing blue gaze on her. "I disagree. We can either talk about it here or up there," he said, nodding toward the loggia and the sound of laughter and conversation.

She stared at him, sure he was bluffing. But just unsure enough she couldn't risk it. Nodding her head, she followed him to a viewing spot near the water that sat under the shade of an enormous plane tree, cut in the shape of a chandelier.

He leaned back against the tree. "You look different. You've cut your hair."

Chiara tipped her chin up. "It was time for a change."

He eyed her, as if assessing the temperature in the air. "You don't love him, Chiara. You don't go from being madly in love with me to madly in love with another man in the space of a few months."

"It's been six months," she said quietly. "And I was never in love with you, Antonio." She knew that now when she compared her feelings for him to the ones she had for Lazzero. "I was *infatuated* with you. Bowled over by your good looks and charm. By the attention and care you lavished on me. I thought I meant something to you. When in reality, I never did."

He rubbed a hand over his jaw. Shook his head. "I *was*

in love with you, Chiara. I told you my marriage to Amalia was a political one. Why can't you get that through your head? Why do you keep pushing me away when we could have something?"

She shook her head, everything crystal clear now. "She is beautiful. Lovely, charming, funny. How can she not be enough for you?"

"Because she isn't you." He fixed his gaze on hers. "You are *alive*. You are fire and passion in bed. You do it for me like no other woman ever has, Chiara."

The blood drained from her face at the blunt confirmation of everything she'd known, but hadn't wanted to believe. "So I was good enough to warm your bed, but I wasn't good enough to stand at your side?"

"It wouldn't have worked," he said quietly. "You know that. I needed the match with Amalia. It works. But I hadn't given up on you. I thought you'd be over it by now. I was going to come see you next month in New York when I'm there."

"Save yourself the trouble." Her chin lifted as she slammed the door shut on that piece of her life with devastating finality. "I am in love with Lazzero, Antonio. I am marrying him. We are *over*."

"You don't mean that," he countered, his dark gaze flashing. "You're hurt. A ring on your finger isn't going to increase your value, Chiara. Not to a man like Di Fiore. You'll still be a possession to him. What's the difference if you're his or mine?"

It stung, as if he'd taken a hand to her face. "He is ten times the man you are," she said flatly, refusing to show him how much it hurt. "You can't even make the comparison. And you're wrong, I do care about him."

Which was scarily, undeniably true.

Frustration etched a stormy path across Antonio's handsome face. "What do you want me to do, Chiara? Walk away from Amalia? You know I can't do that."

Her heart tipped over and tumbled to her stomach. He actually *believed* she still wanted him after everything he'd done?

"I want you to leave me alone," she said harshly. "I want you to forget we ever existed."

"Chiara—"

She turned on her heel and walked away.

Lazzero emerged from his after-dinner chat with Gianni infuriated by the Italian's perpetual game of hard to get. Now that he and the Fiammata CEO were aligned when it came to the design sensibility of a potential Supersonic Volare line, Gianni had turned his focus to price and how much he expected to be compensated for Volare. Which was astronomical—far more than Lazzero had offered—and also utterly ridiculous for a single piece of intellectual property.

Firmly immersed in the black mood that had overtaken him, he sought out Chiara. When she wasn't in the group enjoying after-dinner drinks, he looked for her downstairs, concerned she wasn't well. He was about to give up, thinking they'd missed one another, when he found her in one of the viewing areas that overlooked the lake. With Antonio Fabrizio, who hadn't taken his eyes off her all dinner, a liberty he had been content to allow because Chiara was beautiful and he couldn't fault Fabrizio for thinking so.

Tempering his rather insanely possessive streak when it came to Chiara, he started toward the two of them, only to have Chiara turn on her heel and walk toward him, her face set in a look of determination.

"Whoa." He settled his hands on her waist as she nearly walked through him. She blinked and looked up. "Sorry," she muttered, an emotion he couldn't read flaring in her green eyes. "I didn't see you there."

He tipped her chin up with his fingers. "You okay? You look pale."

She nodded. Waved a hand toward Fabrizio, who was making his way up the stairs. "Antonio was just showing me his boat. The *Amalia*. It's quite something."

He studied the play of emotion in her eyes. "You sure?"

"Yes. I am tired though. Do you think we can leave soon?"

Her request mirrored his own desire to end the evening before he self-combusted. Setting a hand to her back, he guided her upstairs where they made a round of goodbyes and said thank you to the Casales.

It was dark on the boat trip back across the lake. This time, he spent the journey focusing on getting them safely back to shore rather than putting his hands on Chiara, doing the same on the stretch of highway back to Milan. She was quiet the whole way, perhaps suffering from the headache Amalia had given her aspirin for. Which worked for him, because he needed to get his antagonism with Gianni out of his system.

Curving a hand around her bare thigh, he focused on the road. Thought about how easy the silences were between them. How easy it was to be with *her*.

She was smart as he'd known, talented as he'd come to find out and compelling in a way he couldn't describe— the most fascinating mix of innocence, toughness and a fierce strength he loved. With more secrets hidden beneath those protective layers, he suspected, glancing over at her shadowed face in the dim light of the car. He shouldn't want to uncover them as much as he did, but the desire was undeniable.

When they arrived back to the Orientale forty-five minutes later, he threw his jacket over a chair and followed Chiara into the dressing room where she stood removing her jewelry. Their sexy moment on the boat infiltrating his head, he came to a halt behind her. Set his hands to her voluptuous hips, his mouth to her throat. "Head better?"

She nodded. Tipped her head back to give him better access, an instinctive response he liked. He pressed a kiss to the sensitive spot between her neck and shoulder. Registered the delicate shiver that went through her.

He should really go work. Crunch some numbers to try and make Gianni's preposterous demands make sense, but he'd been so hot for her from the moment they'd stepped off that boat tonight, he needed to have her. And maybe once he had, he could pry what was wrong out of her in bed. *Fix it.*

He pulled her back against him so she could feel his arousal pressed against her. Her heady gasp made him smile. With a sigh, she melted back into him, the bond between them undeniable. *Incomparable.*

He scraped his teeth across the pulse pounding at the base of her throat. Slid a hand inside the wrap front of her dress and curved it possessively around her breast. Her little moans as he stroked the silky button to an erect peak had him hard as titanium. Setting his hands on her thighs, he slid them up underneath the sleek material of her dress until he found the soft skin of her upper thighs.

"God," he murmured, his mouth against her throat. "You make me so hot for you, Chiara. Like no other woman has... I can't think when I'm around you."

She went stiff as a board. "What did you just say?"

He paused. Racked his brain, numbed with lust. "I said you make me hot for you. Like no other woman does. It's true. You do."

She pulled out of his arms and swung to face him so fast it made his head spin. Set a smoldering green gaze on his. "I am more than just an *object*, Lazzero."

He eyed her warrior pose, arms crossed over her chest, cheeks flushed with arousal. "Of course you are. You know I appreciate everything about you."

Her mouth set in an uncertain line. He swore and shoved his hands in his pockets which only increased his agony. His mother had perfected the hot and cold routine. He'd watched his father spin like a hamster on a wheel trying to keep up. He was *not* doing this tonight. No matter how much he wanted her.

He dug his fingers into the knot of his tie, stripped it off and tossed it on the armoire. "I need to work," he bit out. "Get some sleep. We can talk in the morning."

He saw the hurt flash through those beautiful eyes. Steeled himself against it as he turned on his heel and left. Which was the sane thing to do, because lust was one thing. Getting emotionally involved with her another thing entirely. Particularly when he had already gone way too far down that path.

Chiara paced the terrace, her thoughts funneling through her head fast and hard, like a tornado on rapid approach. Lazzero had requested honesty at the start of all of this. She should tell him. *But why?* her brain countered. Antonio wasn't anyone's business but her own. She'd made it clear it was over a long time ago. It was Antonio's problem if he couldn't accept it. It *was* history. What use would it be to dredge it up?

She kept pacing under the luminous hanging hook of a moon, a tight knot forming in her chest. She and Lazzero *had* something—a fledgling bond they were building she was afraid to break. She'd felt it on that boat tonight. She was falling for him and she thought he might feel something for her too. Unless she was reading him all wrong, she conceded, which she could be because she'd done it before.

Would he understand if she told him the truth about Antonio? Or would he judge her for being as naive as she'd undoubtedly been when it came to him?

There didn't seem to be a right answer. Lost in a circular

storm of confusion, she finally went inside, removed her makeup and stood under a long, hot shower in the steam room, hoping it would ease the tension in her body and provide clarity to the questions racing through her head. But she only felt worse as she dried herself off and put on her pajamas.

She had completely overreacted to what Lazzero had said. Had allowed her history with Antonio to rule her when Lazzero had proven every which way but Sunday how highly he thought of her. And here she was, ruining it all.

She curled up in the big, king-size bed in the shadow of the beautiful silver moon. But her heart hurt too much to sleep.

Lazzero went over his financials in the study. But no matter which way he spun the numbers, they simply didn't make sense. Which left him in an impossible position. Pay more for Volare than it was worth and put Supersonic's growth in jeopardy, or walk away from the deal and admit to the analysts who ruled his future he had been too hasty in his predictions for that rapid growth he'd promised, an admission—as Santo had stated so bluntly—they would crucify him for.

Neither of which he considered options. Which left his only choice to call Gianni's bluff and force him to make a deal. Which wasn't at all a sure bet given the competitors the Italian CEO had hinted he had waiting in the wings—a British sportswear giant the one that worried him the most.

Painted into a corner of his own making, he pushed to his feet, poured himself a glass of whiskey and carried it to the floor-to-ceiling windows that overlooked the city. Gianni he would solve. He was banking on the fact that there wasn't a company in America right now hotter than Supersonic. That the Fiammata CEO was so enamored of his dominant US market share, his offer would outshine the others.

Chiara, on the other hand, was a puzzle he couldn't seem to decipher. The scene they'd just acted out was a perfect demonstration of everything he'd spent his life avoiding. Exactly what happened when you got invested in someone. It got messy. *Complicated.*

Except, he conceded, taking a sip of the whiskey, Chiara was different. She wasn't a practiced manipulator like his mother had been, nor was she a drama queen like Carolina. She was honest and transparent—real in a way he'd never encountered. And something was wrong.

Sure, he might have needed to blow off some steam tonight, but she had never been an object to him. *Ever.* And she knew it. She had been just as into him on that boat tonight as he had been to her, her reaction to him in the dressing room way off.

He polished off the Scotch, battling his inner instincts as he did so. He should stay away. He knew it. But his inability to remain detached from Chiara was a habit he couldn't seem to break.

The bedroom was plunged into darkness when he walked in, the glow of the moon its only light, spilling through the windows and splashing onto the silk-covered bed. Chiara was curled up in it on her side of the mattress, but he could tell she wasn't sleeping from the rhythm of her breathing. Shucking all of his clothes except his boxers, he slid into bed.

Silence.

Sighing at the tension that stretched between them, he reached for her, curving an arm around her waist and pulling her into his warmth. *"Mi dispiace,"* he murmured, pressing a kiss against her shoulder. "I am in a filthy mood because of Gianni. He has me running in circles."

Chiara twisted in his arms to face him. Propped herself

up on her elbow. "No—" she said on a halting note, "—it was me. I let my baggage get the better of me. I'm sorry. It wasn't fair to you."

Dark hair angled across her face, skin bare of makeup, eyes glittering like twin emerald pools, she was impossible to resist. He ran a finger down her flushed cheek. "How about you tell me what happened earlier? Because I don't think that was about *us* and what we have here."

An emotion he couldn't read flickered through those beautiful eyes before she dropped back onto the pillow and fixed her gaze on the ceiling. "It's hard to explain."

"Try," he invited.

She waved a hand at him. "It's always been about the way I look. Ever since high school. While the girls were making fun of my clothes, the boys wanted me for what was underneath them, which only made the girls more vicious to me. I didn't know how to handle it, so I retreated. Which was fine, because mostly, I was at home with my father. But also because I didn't trust. I didn't believe anyone would want me for who I was, so it was easier that way."

"Then," she said, twisting a lock of her hair around her finger, "I finally met someone that I thought did. I opened myself up to him. Trusted him. Only to realize he had no intentions of letting me share his life. He only wanted me in his bed." She pursed her lips. "What you said tonight reminded me of him. Of something he said."

His heart turned over. He'd known that son of a bitch had done a number on her. He'd like to find him and take him apart piece by piece. But hadn't he objectified her too with his offer to come to Italy? With his suggestion he *gloss her up*? To make her fit into his world? Except he'd always seen more in Chiara than just her undeniably beautiful packaging. Had always known there *was* more to her if he could just manage to peel back those layers of hers. And he'd been right.

He caught her hand in his. Uncurled her tight fingers to lace them through his own. "You know I care about you," he said gruffly. Because he did and he wanted her to know that.

She nodded. Eyed him silently.

"What?"

"Gianni," she murmured. "You're letting him make you crazy, Lazzero. Why not develop the technology yourself if he's going to be like this?"

The far too perceptive question stirred the frustration lurking just beneath the surface. "Because I don't have the time," he said evenly, tempering his volatile edge. "Acquiring Volare means we can put the shoe into production immediately. Meet our steep growth trajectory."

"And if Gianni won't sell it to you? What do you do then?"

A muscle jumped in his jaw. "I'll cross that bridge when and if we come to it."

"Maybe," she suggested quietly, "if Gianni *doesn't* work out, it's time to get back to your roots. To make it about the passion again."

He arched a brow. "Who says the passion's missing?"

"I do." She shook her head. "I saw your face at Di Fiore's that night, Lazzero, when you talked about starting Supersonic. How you came alive when we were doing those sketches... You say you don't dream anymore, but you and Santo *had* a dream to make the best products out there for athletes. Because you *are* athletes. Because it's in your blood. *That* is what you should be doing. Not running circles around Gianni Casale."

"It's not that simple," he said curtly. "Dreams grow up. I run a multibillion-dollar business, Chiara. I've made promises to my shareholders I need to keep. This isn't about sitting down in the lab with my engineers playing house. It's about making my numbers."

Her chin lifted. "I'm not talking about playing house. I'm talking about following your passion, just as you've been pushing me to do." She waved a hand at him. "I've been thinking a lot about what you said this week. About what I want out of life. Sometimes dreams *are* too expensive to keep. And sometimes they're all you have."

And now she was threatening to blow up his brain. "I don't need a lecture right now," he said softly, past the shimmering red in his head. "I need some sleep. Tomorrow's a big day."

"Fine." She lay there staring at the ceiling.

He let out a pained sound. "What?"

"I just think if you dish it out, you should be able to take it."

His blood sizzled in his veins. "Oh, I can take it," he purred, eyes on her pajamas, which tonight, had big red kisses plastered across them. "But I'm trying to keep my hands off you at the moment. At *your* request."

Her white incisors bit into her lip, her eyes big as they rested on his. "I thought you wouldn't be in the mood now."

The vulnerable, hesitant look on her face hit him square in the solar plexus. "Baby," he murmured, "if there's a planet in this solar system where I wouldn't want you in that outfit, you're going to have to find it for me."

A river of color spread across her face, a smoky heat darkening her gaze. "Lazzero—" she breathed, her eyes on his.

He pushed a hand into the bed and brought himself down over her. Bracing himself on his palms and knees, he lowered his mouth to her ear. "Say it," he murmured, "and I will."

And so she did, whispering her request for him to make love to her in a husky voice that unearthed a whole new set of foreign emotions inside of him. Ones he had no idea how to verbalize. And then, because actions had always spoken louder than words and he wanted to show her what she did to him, *on every level*, he deified her instead.

Caging her sexy, amazing body with his, he moved his mouth over every centimeter of her satiny skin until her pajamas impeded his progress and he stripped those off too. Exploring every dip and curve, he trailed his mouth over the taut, trembling skin of her abdomen, found the delectable crease between hip and thigh.

Chiara sucked in a breath, fisted her hands in the bedspread. He could tell she loved it when he did this to her. It made her wild for him. But she was also at her most vulnerable—stripped open and exposed to him. And that was exactly the way he wanted her right now. He wanted to obliterate the distance she'd put between them earlier and put them back exactly where they belonged.

He spread her thighs with firm hands. Slid a palm beneath her bottom and lifted her up to him. Her delicate, musky scent made his head spin. He blew a heated breath over her most intimate flesh. Felt her thighs quiver. Heard the rush of air that left her lips. It set his blood on fire.

He explored her first with his mouth and then with his fingers, caressing every pleasure point with a reverent touch. Her tiny whimpers of pleasure, the clutch of her fingers in his hair, threatened to incinerate him.

"Look at me." His throaty voice dragged her out of the vortex, her eyes stormy and hazy as they focused on his. "When you are like this, stripped bare, Chiara, when you allow yourself to be *vulnerable*, you are insanely beautiful."

Her eyes darkened. Drifted shut. He spread her wider with his hands. Feasted on her, devoured her until she was shaking beneath him. He had meant to dismantle her. Instead he dismantled himself as he mercilessly ended it with the hard pull of his mouth on the most sensitive part of her. It tore a cry from her throat, her broken release reverberating through him.

His skin on fire, his heart pounding in his chest, he crawled up her sated, limp body, clasped her arms above her head and, his hands locked with hers, took her in a slow, sweet possession that lasted forever.

Something locked into place as he watched her shatter alongside him. A piece of him he'd never accessed before. A piece of himself he hadn't known existed. He thought it might be the point of no return.

She fell asleep in his arms, her dark lashes fanning her cheeks. He held her, his breath ruffling the silky hair that slid across her cheek. But sleep eluded him, what she'd said about Gianni turning through his head. Maybe because he thought there might be a grain of truth in what she'd said. That he *had* lost his passion somewhere along the way and it had become all about the business. That all he *knew* was how to keep on pushing, because what would he find if he stopped?

CHAPTER TEN

WITH A HEART-STOPPING Americas team win—the first ever for the squad—in the history books at La Coppa Estiva that afternoon, Chiara dressed for the closing party amidst a buoyant air of celebration. To be held at one of the swishest hotels in the city, it was pegged to be the bash of the year.

Smoothing her palms over her hips, she surveyed her appearance in the black oak mirror in the dressing room at the Orientale. She'd spent far too long choosing her dress, vacillating between the two choices Micaela had given her until she'd finally settled on a round-necked, sleeveless cream sheath that showed off the olive tone of her skin and made the most of her figure.

She thought Lazzero would appreciate the sexy slit that came to midthigh. Which was going to be the *last* time she allowed herself to think like that, because tomorrow it was back to reality. Back to their respective lives. And maybe, if everything worked out with Bianca, exciting new possibilities for her. Hoping for more with Lazzero, when she knew his capabilities, would be a fool's errand. Asking for a broken heart.

Except, she conceded, her heart sinking, it might already be too late. That somewhere along the way, the charade had faded and reality had ensued and this relationship had morphed into something exciting and real and she *didn't* want it to end.

If her head told her it was impossible to fall in love with someone so quickly, her heart told her otherwise.

As if she'd summoned him with her thoughts, Lazzero blew into the dressing area, a towel wrapped around his hips, a frown marring his brow. Clearly used to maximizing every minute of the day, he went straight for the wardrobe.

Her eyes moved over his shoulders and biceps bulging with thick muscle, down over abs that looked as if they'd been carved out of rock, to the mouthwatering, V-shaped indentation that disappeared beneath the towel. He was the hottest man she'd ever encountered. Being with him had been the most breathtakingly exciting experience of her life. But he was so much more than that, the glimpses he'd given her into the man that he was making her want *more* of him, not less.

He shot her a distracted glance. "Do you have any idea where Edmondo put the shirt to my tux?"

"In the far closet," she said huskily. "Closest to the door."

He stalked over to the closet. Snared the shirt off the hanger. "*Perfetto.* Now if I can just find my bow tie, we're in business."

She pointed to a drawer. He bent and rustled through it, straightening with the black tie in his hand, a victorious look on his face. "Amazing. How did I ever do this without you?"

She couldn't actually answer that because he'd been serious all day. Too serious, avoiding any kind of personal interaction after that amazing night they'd shared. Except when she'd literally forced him onto the bed to ice his knee after he'd limped away from today's brutally physical match. His eyes had turned to flame then, a suggestion she could ease his pain in another way entirely rolling off his tongue. To which she'd replied they had no time.

And now he was back to serious. As if maybe he'd rethought everything, decided she'd been exactly the kind of high-maintenance female he avoided like the plague last night and it was best to dump her before they got back to New York.

She couldn't read him *at all*. It was making her a little crazy.

Lazzero shifted his distracted survey to her. "You okay?"

She nodded.

"Bene." A smile creased his cheeks. "You look incredible. I'll be ready in five."

The crowds were thick outside the Bvlgari Hotel, located in a renovated, eighteenth-century Milanese palazzo just around the corner from the Orientale. There was that same intimidating red carpet to walk, that same unnerving need to be *on*, but tonight Chiara was too distracted to pay it much heed, relying on the hand Lazzero had resting on the curve of her back to guide her through the throngs of guests and hangers-on.

The party was in full swing in the meticulously landscaped gardens where trees and hedges created a series of open-air rooms. Lit in La Coppa Estiva blue, the buoyant crowd was buzzing under the influence of one of Italy's most famous DJs, a celebratory atmosphere in the air. Soon, she and Lazzero were caught up in it, acquiring glasses of the champagne that was flowing like water while they made the rounds.

The only minor ripple in the celebration was the appearance of Antonio as he worked the party with his international contacts, minus Amalia who had come down with a cold. Chiara blew off his attempt to talk to her when Lazzero was waylaid by Carolina and one of the other organizers, and determinedly ignored him from that point on.

Pia, accompanied by a surly Valentino, who'd been a part of the losing team, soon came up to whisk her off to the dance floor.

"I need you," Pia said. "He's making me crazy."

Chiara smiled. Looked up at Lazzero. "Okay?"

"Yes," he drawled, subjecting her to one of those looks that could strip the paint from a car. "But don't go far. I need to be able to look at you in that dress."

A flush stained her skin as he bent to brush a kiss against her cheek. *"Go."*

She frowned as he straightened, visibly favoring his left leg. "You should stay off that knee."

"And how," he murmured, dropping his mouth to her ear, "will I get you to play nursemaid if I do?"

"You don't need a nursemaid," she said saucily. "You need to be able to walk tomorrow."

Lazzero watched as Chiara turned on her heel and followed Pia into the crowd. He couldn't take his eyes off her in that dress. The sleek design molded her fabulous figure like a glove and the slit that left an expanse of silky skin bare every time she moved was an invitation to sin.

His head fully immersed in the woman who had just walked away from him, it took him a moment to realize Santo had materialized at his side, sharp in black Armani.

"Sorry?" he said on a distracted note. "What did you say?"

"I said, 'Well if it isn't the man of the hour...'" Santo clapped him on the back. "That was a genius of a final play, *fratello*. Aren't you glad you played?"

Lazzero muttered something in the affirmative. Santo eyed him, a glitter in his eyes. *"Dannazione."*

"What?"

"The dark knight has fallen."

"What the hell are you talking about?"

"Her." Santo nodded at Chiara's retreating figure. "Your barista. You are ten feet under. *Fully brewed.* In case you hadn't noticed."

He had. He just had no idea what the hell to do about it. He'd been thinking about it all night. He should let Chiara walk away. Call it a scorching-hot affair done right. Nobody gets hurt. Everybody wins. *His specialty*. Because Chiara didn't play by the same rules as him. And maybe that was the real reason he'd stayed away from her as long as he had.

And then he'd invited her to come to Italy with him. Had kissed her, made love to her and crossed every line in the book. Which left him exactly where?

"I need a drink," he said flatly.

"A celebratory drink," Santo agreed.

Ensconcing themselves at the bar, they exchanged their fruity glasses of champagne for an excellent measure of off-list smoky bourbon as they recapped the game in glorified detail.

It hit him like a knife edge how much he'd missed the adrenaline that had once been his lifeblood. The *buzz* that came from being on the firing line in a pivotal match.

Competition was in his blood—it was what he thrived on. The *purpose* that had once fueled his days, because if he'd been on the court nothing else had mattered.

Building Supersonic had fulfilled that competitive edge. The need to *conquer*. But somewhere along the way the rush had faded. Carrying the weight of a team, of a school, on his back might rival the necessity to keep ten thousand people in a job, but his soul wasn't in it the way it had once been. Chiara had been right about that.

He watched her on the dance floor with Pia. Wondered what it was about her he couldn't resist. She was beautiful, yes. But he'd dated scores of beautiful women. Chiara was *real* in a way he'd never encountered before. She challenged him, made him think. He was *better* when he was with her. Happy even, a descriptor he would never have used with himself.

If the truth be known, he went into that damn café every

morning because he wanted to see her. Because he didn't feel half-alive when he was around her. And the thought of them going back to the status quo with Chiara serving him an espresso in the morning with one of those cool, controlled expressions on her face made him a little nuts. But what, exactly, did he have to offer her?

She deserved someone who would be there for her. An *Alfredo*. Someone who would offer her that true love she was looking for. Someone who would be that solid force she needed to shine. Who would prove to her she would always be *enough*.

Which was not him. He had never been *that guy*. So why the hell did he want to be so badly?

When he couldn't help himself any longer, he left his brother to the devices of a beautiful redhead and sought Chiara out on the dance floor.

Chiara tipped her head back to look up at Lazzero as they danced, her pulse racing at the banked heat in his gaze. He'd been staring at her the whole time she'd been on the dance floor with Pia, his desire for her undeniable. But maybe, she acknowledged, a hand fisting her chest, that was all it was.

He slid a hand to her hip in a possessive hold. Tugged her closer. "Do you know what I was thinking the opening night when I was holding you like this?"

"What?"

"That I wanted to ditch the party and have you until the sun came up." His gaze darkened. "I am crazy about you, Chiara. You know that I am."

Her heart missed a beat. She'd been so scared she'd been imagining it. Building it up in her head like she'd done before. Getting it all wrong. "You don't want to end this when we get back to New York?"

He shook his head. "I think we should see each other

back in New York. See where this goes. If," he qualified quietly, "you want that too."

She sank her teeth into her lip. "What do you mean, 'see where this goes'?"

"I mean exactly that. We explore what we have. See where it takes us." He shook his head. "I'm not good at this, Chiara. I could mess it up. But I don't want to lose you. *That*, I know."

Her knees went weak. He wasn't making any promises. She could end up with her heart broken all over again. Was likely setting herself up for it. But everything she'd learned about Lazzero made her think he was worth it. That if she was patient, she might be able to breach those tightly held defenses of his. That maybe she could be *the one*.

A whisper of fear fluttered through her belly at the thought of making herself that vulnerable again. Because Lazzero, she knew, could annihilate her far worse than Antonio had ever done. But the chance to have him, to *be* with him, to hold on to that solid force he'd become for her, was far too tempting to resist.

She stood on tiptoe and kissed him by way of response. A long, slow shimmer of a connection, it was perfection. But soon it grew hungrier, *needier*, the flames between them igniting.

Lazzero enclosed the nape of her neck with his hand and took the kiss deeper, delving into her mouth in a hot, languid joining that stole her breath. She settled her palms on his chest. Grabbed a handful of his shirt. Every hot breath, every stroke, every lick, sensual, earthy, built the flames higher.

Tracing a path across her jaw and down to the hollow of her throat, Lazzero pressed an openmouthed kiss to her pulse. It was racing like a jackhammer. He flicked his tongue across the frantic beat, shifted his hands lower to shape her against his hard male contours. A gasp slipped from her lips.

He pulled back. Surveyed her kiss-swollen mouth. "I think this time we *are* leaving," he murmured. "The song's over, *caro*. Go get your things."

Lazzero propped himself up against the bar while Chiara collected her wrap, a supreme feeling of satisfaction settling over him. He was strategizing on all the different ways he would take her apart until she begged for him, when Antonio Fabrizio slid into place beside him at the bar and ordered a Scotch. Turning to face the Italian, he reluctantly switched back into networking mode.

"Enjoying yourself?" he murmured lazily.

"Sì." Fabrizio reclined his lanky frame against the bar, his gaze on Chiara's retreating figure. "Beautiful, isn't she? The most beautiful woman in the room, no doubt."

Lazzero stood up straighter. "I think so," he agreed evenly. "But then again, she's my fiancée, so I would."

"Still," the Italian drawled, "a man would be hard-pressed to resist."

And now he'd had it. Lazzero's blood sizzled, the amount of bourbon warming his blood doing little to leash his temper. He'd been okay with the man admiring Chiara last night, but really, enough was enough. Given, however, Gianni had let it slip that the Fabrizio investment house was one of Fiammata's largest stakeholders, he needed to keep it civil.

"Luckily," he said icily, "I don't have to." He waved a hand at the other man. "I have a suggestion, Fabrizio. You have a beautiful wife. Perhaps you should go home and lavish some attention on her."

The Italian lifted a shoulder. "Amalia is a political match. Unexciting in bed. Chiara, on the other hand, is not."

Lazzero froze. *"Scusi?"*

Fabrizio set a cold, blue gaze on him. "You didn't know? She was mine before she was yours, Di Fiore. Or didn't she tell you that?"

He was lying, was his first thought. But he had no reason to lie. Which meant he was the one in the dark here.

"When?" he grated.

Fabrizio shrugged. "It ended before Christmas. I was engaged to Amalia. Chiara didn't like playing, what do you Americans call it...*second fiddle* to my fiancée, so she broke it off. Gave me an ultimatum—it was Amalia or her." The Italian tipped his glass at Lazzero. "As far as her being in love with you? Highly unlikely given she made a habit of telling me she was in love with me every morning before I left for work."

Lazzero's head snapped back. Fabrizio was telling him he'd had an affair with Chiara months ago? A man she'd calmly pretended she'd never met last night when they'd been introduced. An *engaged man*.

Except she hadn't been calm, he recalled. She'd been off from the moment Antonio Fabrizio had shown up at that party. Had blown off his concern for her as a case of fatigue. His brain putting two and two together, he rocked back on his heels. Fabrizio was the man who'd broken her heart?

A dangerous red settled over his vision. He had just poured out his feelings to her. Had just told her he was crazy about her. And she had lied to his face. Did he even *know* her?

"I get it," Fabrizio murmured. "She's *insano* in bed. Almost worth putting a four-carat ring on her finger."

It was the "almost worth it" that did it. Lazzero had Fabrizio by the collar of his bespoke suit before he knew what he was doing. Blind fury driving him, he balled his hand into a fist and sent it flying toward the Italian's face. Anticipating the supreme satisfaction of watching it connect with that arrogant, square jaw, he found his hand manacled just short of its destination.

"What the hell are you doing?" Santo said, wrapping an arm around him and hauling him backward. "Have you lost your mind?"

Fabrizio straightened the lapel of his suit as a shocked crowd looked on. Picked up his Scotch and shifted away from the bar, his eyes on Lazzero. "By the way," he drawled. "I nudged Gianni in the direction of the British deal. It has a more global scope."

His parting volley hanging in the air, the Italian sauntered off into the crowd. Enraged, Lazzero pulled at Santo's grip to follow him, but his brother held him back. Directed a furious look at Lazzero. "What the hell is wrong with you? He's a key stakeholder in Fiammata, for God's sake."

Lazzero shrugged him off. Raked a hand through his hair. "He's an arrogant bastard."

"So you decided to *hit* him?"

A frisson of fury lanced through him. "No," he bit out. "That was for something else."

"Well, whatever it is, you need to get it together. Everything hinges on this deal, Laz. Or have you forgotten?"

Lazzero's mouth thinned. "He baited me."

"Which appears to be your Achilles' heel," his brother observed. "Perhaps food for thought as you do some damage control here."

Chiara claimed her wrap, practically floating on air. A sharp bite of anticipation nipped at her skin as she made her way back through the crowd to where Lazzero was waiting for her at the bar.

Her progress painfully slow, she looked up to catch his eye. Noted he was deep in conversation. The tall, dark male he was talking to shifted to pick up his drink. *Antonio*, she registered. Which would have been fine. A social chat perhaps. *Business*. Except for the expression on Lazzero's face. *Oh, my God.*

Heart pounding, she quickened her pace, desperate to intervene. But the crowd was too tightly packed, her high heels allowing her to move only so fast. By the time she made it to the bar, Santo was hauling Lazzero away from Antonio after some type of an altercation. Antonio, who looked utterly unruffled, straightened his suit, said something to Lazzero, then melted off into the crowd.

She came to a sliding halt in front of the two brothers. Santo said something to Lazzero, a heated look on his face, then stalked off. He looked just as furious as his brother. *Or maybe not.* Lazzero looked *livid*.

"What happened?" she breathed.

Lazzero's face was a wall of concrete. "We are not talking about it here."

She didn't argue because the rage coming off him in waves was making her knees weak. Clutching her purse to her side, she practically ran to keep up with his long strides as they found Carolina and the other organizers of the party, thanked them, then walked the couple of blocks back to their hotel.

When they entered their suite, Lazzero peeled off his jacket and threw it on a chair. Whipping off his bow tie, he tossed it on top of his jacket and walked to the bar to pour himself a drink. Carrying the glass to the windows, he stood looking out at a shimmering view of a night-lit Milan.

Chiara kicked off her heels and threw her wrap on a chair. Her throat too tight to get words past it, her brain rifled through the possible scenarios of what had just happened. Which were too varied and scary to consider, so she stood, arms hugged around herself, and waited for Lazzero to speak. Which he finally did.

"Why didn't you tell me about Fabrizio?"

She blanched. Felt the world fall away from beneath her feet. "I didn't think it was anyone's business but my own," she said, managing to find her voice as he turned to face her. "Antonio and I were over months ago. It was history to me. I didn't see the point in bringing it up."

"You didn't see the point?" His voice was so quiet, so cold, it sent a chill through her. "Because you had an affair with a man who *belonged to someone else*?"

The blood drained from her face. "I didn't have an affair with him. I didn't know he was engaged, Lazzero. He lied to me. I told you what happened last night."

"You didn't tell me it was *Antonio Fabrizio!*" He yelled the words at her with such force she took a stumbling step backward. "Fabrizio is one of Fiammata's largest stakeholders, Chiara. There are three, equally strong deals on the table for Volare. That son of a bitch told Gianni to take the British offer over ours."

Oh, good God, no. The blood froze in her veins. She had known Antonio was angry. That he wasn't one to concede defeat. But she'd been so sure the fact that she was engaged to Lazzero would have driven the point home that she was unavailable. Which, she admitted numbly, had been a gross miscalculation on her part.

"I'm so sorry," she said dazedly, sinking down on the arm of the sofa. "I can't believe he did this."

His gaze glittered like hard, polished ebony. "What were you two talking about by the lake, then? If it's *over*?"

She sank her teeth into her lip. "It's complicated."

"Enlighten me," he growled.

She pressed her palms to her cheeks. Dropped her hands to her sides. "I met Antonio at a party last summer in Chelsea. It was a sophisticated crowd—I was completely out of my league. Worried about my father. You know what it's been like. Antonio—he pursued me relentlessly. He wouldn't give up. He swept me off my feet, made all sorts of promises and within weeks we were living together.

"I thought we had something. That he loved me. Until one morning when I was leaving the penthouse for work, I bumped into his mother. She'd come to surprise Antonio for his birthday—to do some Christmas shopping. She told me Antonio had a fiancée in Milan. That I was just his American plaything."

Her stomach curled at the memory. "I was crushed. *Devastated.* I gave Antonio his key back that night and told him I never wanted to see him again. He was furious. Refused to take no for an answer. He kept sending me flowers, theater tickets, jewelry. Kept calling me. I sent it all back, told him I wanted nothing to do with him. Finally, a couple of months ago, he stopped calling."

Lazzero watched her with a hooded gaze. "And last night?"

"Antonio followed me when I went to the washroom. He said he hadn't given up on me. That he thought I'd be over Amalia by now and he was going to come and see me in New York the next time he was in town."

"Because he wants you back."

A statement, not a question. One she couldn't refute, even with the recrimination written across Lazzero's face. "Yes," she admitted. "He wants me to be his mistress. He asked me what I wanted—if I wanted him to leave Amalia, because he couldn't. I told him I was engaged to you. That I loved you. That I wanted him to forget we ever existed, because I want nothing to do with him."

"He *said* you disliked playing second fiddle to Amalia. That you, in effect, had given him an ultimatum—it was her or you."

Her breath left her in a rush. "That's a lie," she rasped. "He is on a seek and destroy mission. If he can't have me, no one will."

"Why bother?" Lazzero murmured. "I get that all men love you, Chiara, but Fabrizio is a powerful man. He could have any woman he wants."

Her stomach curled at the insinuation she wasn't worth pursuing. That she had somehow *invited* Antonio's attention last night. That she was in some way responsible for what had happened.

"Antonio is entitled," she said quietly, fingers clenching at her sides. "He *does* think he can have anything he wants. I think you forget you're the one who walked into the café and threw that insane amount of money at me to come with you, Lazzero. You're the one who wouldn't take no for an answer. *I* never wanted to be any part of this world."

"Because he is here."

"Yes," she snapped back at the look of condemnation in his eyes, "because he is here. I put him out of my life, Lazzero. I had no idea he was married to Amalia. I was in complete shock last night at the dinner party. But never once did I give him any encouragement that there might still be something between us. You know how I feel about you."

"I don't *know* anything," he lanced back. "I have no idea what the hell to believe, because you lied to my face, Chiara." He pointed the Scotch at her. "I gave you every opportunity to tell me what was wrong last night. Every opportunity you needed. And you told me you were tired. That *nothing* was wrong."

Her stomach dropped, like a book toppling off a high shelf. She should have told him. She had known he had trust issues. Had known he'd let down his walls for her. Had known she'd been playing with fire by not telling him. And still, she had done it.

"I was afraid to lose you," she admitted softly. "Afraid you wouldn't understand."

A choked-off sound of disbelief ripped itself from his throat. "So you did the one thing guaranteed to make that happen? *Maledizione*, Chiara. You know my history on this. I thought we *had* something here. I thought we were building something together. I thought we were different."

"We are," she blurted out, her heart in her mouth. "I'm falling for you, Lazzero. You know that."

"How would you even know *who* you're in love with?" He waved a hand at her. "A few months ago it was him. Now it's me. Do you just turn it on and off at will? Like a tap?"

Her stomach contracted at the low blow. At the closed-off look on his face, getting colder by the minute. "I was never in love with him," she said evenly, her chin lifting. "I *thought* I was. How I feel for you is completely different."

He shrugged that off. "Trust was the one thing that was nonnegotiable in this. You knew that."

"Lazzero," she said huskily, "it was an error in judgment. *One* mistake."

"Which could bury me." He raked a hand through his hair. Eyed her. "Is there anything else I should know? Any other powerful men you have slept with who can annihilate my future?"

Her breath caught in her throat. "You did *not* just say that."

He pushed away from the bar and headed for the study. "I need to go research the competition. See if I can salvage this."

The finality of it, the judgment written across his face said it all. Whatever she said, it wasn't going to be enough.

"Why did you try and hit him?" She tossed the question after him because she had to know.

He turned around, mouth twisting. "He suggested you were *almost* worth a four-carat ring. I was defending your honor, fool that I am."

CHAPTER ELEVEN

CHIARA DIDN'T SLEEP. She lay awake all night in the gorgeous four-poster bed, numb, *frozen*, as she waited for Lazzero to join her. But he never did, pulling one of his all-nighters in an attempt to salvage the deal. And what, she conceded miserably, staring up at the beautiful crystal chandelier, would she have even said to him if he had?

She *should* have told him about Antonio. She could never have predicted what Antonio had done—was still in utter shock that he'd done it. But she had known about Lazzero's trust issues. And instead of believing in what they had, in what they were building together, she'd reverted back to her old ways. Had allowed her insecurities to rule. And in doing so, she'd destroyed everything.

Sleepless and bleary-eyed, she boarded the jet for their flight home to New York the following afternoon. Lazzero devoted the entire journey to his effort to discredit his British competition, which left such a sick feeling in her stomach, she hadn't slept there, either.

If she hadn't known it was over the night before, she knew it was when Lazzero bid her a curt farewell on the tarmac, he and Santo en route to a sports fund-raiser, not one speck of that warmth he usually reserved for her in his gorgeous, dark eyes. She gave him back the ring, unable to bear wearing it a moment longer, only to have Lazzero wave his hand at her and tell her to keep it. *He couldn't take it back and she needed the money.*

It had been all she could do not to throw it at him. She told him instead that she couldn't be bought, that she'd never been for sale and shoved the ring in his hand. Then she'd allowed Gareth, whom Lazzero had handed her off to, to shepherd her into the Bentley for the drive home.

Her carpe diem moment seemed foolish as the car slid smoothly off into the night. She had told herself it was a mistake to accept Lazzero's offer. To allow herself to fall for him. Then she'd gone ahead and done it anyway and fool that she'd been, she'd started to buy into the fairy tale. Of what she and Lazzero could be.

Her chest throbbed in a tight, hot ache as the headlights from the other cars slid across her face. She'd opened herself up exactly as Lazzero had challenged her to—had shown him who she truly was—had taken that leap—only to have him walk away as if what they'd shared had meant nothing. As if *she* wasn't worth the effort. Which might hurt the most of all.

The sun was sinking in a giant, red-orange ball when she arrived at her apartment in Spanish Harlem, bidding the city a sultry, crimson adieu. Gareth, a gentleman to the end, helped her up the three sets of stairs to her door and made sure she was safely inside before he melted back into the sunset like the former special agent he likely was.

The apartment was hot and stuffy, empty with Kat working the closing shift. She dumped her suitcase in the living room, too exhausted to even think about unpacking, because then she would have to look at all those beautiful clothes and the memories that came with them. About the man who'd just walked away from her without a backward glance.

She called her father instead as she made a cup of herbal tea, anxious to talk to him after a week of trading messages. Only to find him bubbling over with the news of a visit by the Five Boroughs Angel Foundation the previous afternoon, in which Ferrante's had been the recipient of an angel investment that would cover the bakery's rent for the remainder of the year.

He'd been so happy and relieved, he'd gone over to Frankie DeLucca's to celebrate. It was almost enough to peel away a layer of her misery as she signed off and promised to see her father the following evening.

She carried the tea into the living room, intent on numbing her brain with one of her dancing shows. But the stiflingly hot room felt like a shoebox after the palatial suite at the Orientale, the sound from her downstairs neighbor's TV was its usual intolerably loud level and the window box air conditioner refused to work.

As if nothing has changed. Except everything had. And maybe that's why her chest felt so tight. Because she'd gone to Italy as one person and come back another. Because of Lazzero.

The tears came then, like hot, silent bandits slipping down her cheeks. And once they started, they wouldn't seem to stop. Which was ridiculous, really, because, in the end, what had Lazzero been offering her? The same no-strings-attached arrangement as Antonio had? A few more weeks of being starry-eyed while she fell harder for a man who had a questionable ability to commit?

She staggered to bed, flattened by jetlag. Rose the next morning with a renewed sense of determination. She was tougher than this. She wasn't going to let Lazzero Di Fiore crush her. She was going to go to this coffee with Bianca and *crush it*. Because if there was one thing Lazzero had taught her, it was that she couldn't depend on anyone else to make her dream happen. That had to come from her.

She met Bianca at the Daily Grind before her shift began. A tall, Katharine Hepburn–like bombshell, Bianca was as tough as Lazzero had described, but also inspiring, brilliant and full of amazing ideas as they looked through her portfolio. When Bianca glanced at her bare left hand for what seemed like the fiftieth time, Chiara waved it in the air. "We broke up," she said shortly. "It was all my fault."

It was the same line she used with the girls at the café when Bianca disappeared out the door with a promise to get back to her with the committee's decision. When a week passed with no sign of Lazzero and his habitual order of a double espresso, her heart jumping every time the bell on the door rang, because maybe he would change his mind. Maybe he would apologize. But it never happened.

Eyes trained on his computer screen, Lazzero pulled the coffee that his PA, Enid, had just delivered within striking distance while he scanned the contents of the email he'd just gotten from Gianni. Only to discover the wily Italian had changed the rules of the game. *Again.*

His mind working a mile a minute at the implications of what the Fiammata CEO was proposing, he lifted the espresso to his lips and took a sip. Almost spit it out.

It was the final straw.

"Enid!" he bellowed, pushing to his feet and heading out to Reception, cup in hand. "What the hell is this?" He arched a brow at her. "Do we not have an espresso machine and do you not know how to use it?"

His exceedingly young, ultraefficient PA, who couldn't be more than twenty-five, gave him a wary look as if considering which angle with which to avoid this new threat. "We do," she agreed evenly, "and I do."

"Then maybe you can try again," he suggested, dumping the cup on her desk. "Because this is filth. *F.I.L.T.H.*"

Enid calmly got to her feet, scooped up the cup and headed toward the kitchen. Santo strolled out of his office, a football palmed between his hands. "Jet lag getting to you?" he asked pointedly.

"Gianni," Lazzero muttered. "He just got back to me."

Santo followed him into his office. "What did he say?"

"'After much consideration,' he's decided to split the global rights for Volare. Supersonic is to receive the North American license, Gladiator, the rest-of-world global rights. Provided we are agreeable with the price tag he has attached to the offer."

"Which is?"

Lazzero named the figure.

Santo blinked. "For the North American rights? That would stretch us."

More than stretch them. It would eliminate other growth opportunities he wanted to pursue. *Close doors.* On a bet that Volare would move heaven and earth for them.

He walked to the window. Looked out at a glittering Manhattan, the sun gilding the skyscrapers the palest shade of gold. If America was the land of opportunity, New York was the epitome of the American Dream. He'd seen it from both sides now—knew what it was like to live one step away from the street with a paralyzing fear as your guiding force and what it was like to have it all. How easily it could flip—in the blink of an eye—with one wrong move.

With one mistake.

He locked his jaw, ignoring the pain riding beneath his chest, because *they* were over and he was better off this way. But that didn't mean she hadn't made him think.

"We're not doing it." He turned around and leaned against the sill, his eyes on Santo. "We take the reputational hit. We tell the analysts it's going to take us a bit longer than we anticipated to make it to number two, and we do it ourselves. The way we do it best."

A wealth of emotion flickered through Santo's dark eyes. "There will be a storm. You know that."

He nodded. The investment community *would* crucify them for missing their targets for the first time in the company's history. There would be that analysis their star had risen too far, too fast. But he hadn't created this company to have it ruled by a bunch of number crunchers in their high-priced offices.

He lifted a shoulder. "We ride it out. We were bound to hit one someday."

Santo palmed the football in his hands. "Okay," he said finally, a rueful smile tilting his lips. "We do it ourselves. We go back to our roots. Tell Gianni to go to hell."

His blood buzzed in his veins. It felt *right* for the first time in forever.

Enid came in with the new espresso. Set it on Lazzero's desk and beat a hasty retreat. Santo eyed the coffee. "You going to do something about that?"

"About what?"

"Your barista."

Lazzero scowled. "What makes you think I need to?"

"Because I've never seen two people try *not* to look at each other as hard as you two did on the plane. Because she lights you up in a way I've never seen before. Because you haven't shaved in a week, you look terrible and you're hurting and you won't admit it." Santo crossed his arms over his chest and cocked a brow. "Have I covered it all?"

Quite possibly. Which didn't mean he wasn't still furious with her.

"You're crazy about her," his brother said quietly. "What's the problem?"

What wasn't? That she had violated the one code of honor he lived his life by, the trust he'd needed to convince himself they could be different. That he'd been *all in for her*, confessed his innermost thoughts and feelings to her when she hadn't shown him the same respect? Because it had felt like the most real thing he'd ever had, when in reality it had been as fake as every other relationship he'd known.

He pushed away from the sill and headed toward his desk. "It was never going to work. She was a temporary thing."

"Good to know," Santo said lazily. "Because I think she's amazing and if you don't go after her, I will." His brother gave a laconic shrug. "I'll give her some time to get over your jaded, broken heart, of course, but then I will."

Lazzero had to smother the urge to go for his brother's throat. He knew he was baiting him and still, the soft taunt twisted a knot in his gut.

He missed her. In the morning giving him sass from the espresso machine…when he walked into the penthouse at night, filling his empty spaces…and definitely, plastered across his bed sketching in those sexy pajamas of hers. But trust and transparency were essential to him.

Santo sauntered out of his office wearing a satisfied look, having stirred him up exactly as he'd known he would. He attempted to anesthetize himself with yet more work alongside the weak, tepid garbage Enid had produced yet again, but he couldn't seem to do it.

The first Monday after the Labor Day weekend was always madness at the Daily Grind. The students were back, relentless in their search of a caffeine injection as they juggled an unfamiliar, highly resented wake-up call, while the flashy-suited urban set struggled to get back to reality after a weekend spent in the Hamptons. And then, there was Sivi, currently having a meltdown over her broken romance with a Wall Street banker who'd ended things over the weekend. Chiara had fixed half a dozen of her messed-up orders already, which wasn't helping her ability to cope with the massive lineup spilling out the door.

"You know what I think?" Sivi announced, handing her

three cups marked with orders of questionable reliability. "*I* think Ted has been reading Samara Jones. I think he decided to dump me because the Athertons' pool party was on the weekend. I was just a *summer shag*. I looked good in a *bathing suit*."

Kat snorted as she made change for a customer. "Men have been systematically dumping women in Manhattan for little to no reason since the beginning of time. The whole concept of a summer shag is ridiculous."

"Oh, it's a real thing," interjected a twentysomething-blonde regular in the lineup. "The event I held last week? Seventy-five percent of the men came with a plus one. My Fall Extravaganza in a couple of weeks? *Fifty percent.*"

"It's an epidemic," said her friend, a perky, blue-eyed brunette. "My roommate found her kiss-off gift in his underwear drawer over the weekend. She's trying to decide whether to stick around or not."

"At least she got a kiss-off gift," grumbled Sivi. "I loved him, I mean, I really *loved him*, you guys. The BlackBerry in bed? No problem. Football all Sunday? I did my nails. And the snoring? It was like the 6-train coming through the walls. But I excused it all for him because he was *just that good in bed.*"

Oh, my God. Chiara wanted to put her head in her hands, but she had two espressos and an Americano to make, and now a frowning customer was shoving her drink back across the counter. "This is *not* what I ordered. I ordered a *triple venti, half-sweet, nonfat caramel macchiato.*"

Chiara counted to five. Sivi waved a cup in the air. "Are there *any* men left in Manhattan who have serious intentions when it comes to a woman?"

"I do," intoned a husky, lightly accented voice. "Although I might have gone about it the wrong way."

Chiara's heart lurched. She looked up to find the owner of that sexy, familiar voice standing in the lineup, all eyes on him as he answered Sivi's question. Which might also have something to do with the way Lazzero looked. Dressed in a severely cut pinstripe suit, a snowy-white shirt and a dark tie, he was so sinfully good-looking, she could only clutch the cup in her hand and stare, her brain cells fried with the pleasure and pain of seeing him again.

She'd missed him. God, she'd missed him.

Memories of their last meeting bled through. She pulled in air through a chest so tight it hurt to breathe. Lowered her gaze and started remaking the macchiato with hands that shook, because he was not doing this. He was damn well not doing this right here and right now.

But, oh, yes, he was. "I am guilty," Lazzero said evenly, "of being *that guy.* Of callously discarding a woman without a second thought. Of believing a piece of jewelry could buy a weekend in the Hamptons. Of thinking my money could acquire anything I wanted."

The perky brunette drank him in from the tip of his sleek, dark head to his custom-made Italian shoes. "I can't say I would have said no."

"Until," Lazzero continued, his eyes on Chiara, "I met the one woman who was immune to it. Who convinced me that I was *wrong.* That I wanted more. And then I was scrambling," he admitted. "I tried every which way but Sunday to show her how different the man was beneath the suit. And then, when I finally did, I screwed it up."

Chiara's stomach swooped, skimming the shiny surface of the bronze, tiled floor. She set the cup down before she dumped espresso all over herself. Took in Lazzero, intensely private Lazzero, who was loath to talk about his feelings, talking to her as if there was no one else in the room. Except the entire front half of the lineup was watching them now and the café had gone strangely silent.

"We are over," she said quietly. "You made that very clear, Lazzero."

"It was a mistake." A stubborn strength underlaid his tone. "You need to give me another chance."

Like he had her? She dumped the misguided macchiato in the sink, her heart shattering all over again at how completely he'd taken her apart. "I don't *need* to do anything. I no longer make coffee on command for you, Lazzero. I no longer serve as your decorative piece on the side and I definitely don't have to forgive you so that I can once again become as expendable as one of your high-priced suits."

"I'm not interested in having you on a temporary basis," Lazzero said huskily, stepping over to the counter. "I'm interested in having you forever. I walked away from the deal, Chiara. Nothing is right without you."

She stared at him, stunned. *He'd walked away from the deal? Why would he do that?* She noted the dark shadows in his eyes then, the white lines bracketing his mouth, the dark stubble on his jaw. Not cool, collected Lazzero. Another version entirely.

"I'm in love with you, Chiara." He trained his gaze on hers. "Give me another chance."

"I don't know about you," said the brunette, "but he had me at the pinstriped suit."

"Yes, but it was necessary to make him grovel," said the blonde. "Not that we know what he did."

Chiara's heart was too busy melting into the floor at the naked emotion blazing in Lazzero's eyes to pay them much heed.

"And now that we have that decided," said a disgruntled-looking construction worker at the front of the line, "could we please have some coffee here? Some of us have to work for a living."

Chiara stared blankly at the drink orders in front of her. Kat waved a hand at her. "*Go.* You are clearly now useless, as well. Sivi—you're on the bar with Tara. And for heaven sakes, try and get it right."

Chiara had to run to keep up with Lazzero when he took her hand and dragged her out of the café and into the bright morning sunshine. Breathless, she leaned against the brick wall of the coffee shop and stared dazedly up at him. "Did you mean that? That you love me?"

"Yes," he said, setting a palm against the wall beside her. "Although the speech was not intentional. You have a way of provoking a completely irrational response in me."

Happiness bloomed inside of her, a dangerous, insidious warmth that threatened to envelop her completely. She bit her lip, held it in check. "What do you mean you walked away from the deal? Why would you do that?"

"Because you were right. Because somewhere along the way, I *had* lost my passion and I needed to get it back. It's what gets me out of bed in the morning. Or *in it* at night," he murmured, his eyes on her mouth. "Which has also been extremely empty. Too empty because I'd let the best thing that's ever happened to me walk out of my life."

The blaze of warmth in his eyes threatened to throw her completely off balance. She spread her palms against the warm brick wall and steeled herself against the desire to throw herself in his arms. "You hurt me with those things you said, Lazzero. Badly."

"I know." He traced the back of his knuckles across her cheek. "And, I'm sorry. If I had been in my right mind, I would have seen the truth. That Antonio had made a wrong decision in letting you go and was doing everything he could to get you back. Instead, I let him push all my buttons. I was blind with jealousy. I thought you might still love him, because he is clearly still in love with you. And I was angry," he allowed, "because I thought what we had was real."

"It *was* real. I should have trusted you, but you needed to trust me too, Lazzero. It goes both ways."

"Yes," he agreed, "but in the moment, that breach of

trust confirmed everything I thought I knew about relation-ships—that they are messy, complicated things better off avoided. Proved us as false as every other relationship in my life had been. That I was the fool, because there I was, letting a woman play with my head, exactly as my father had done time and time again."

Her stomach curled. "I wish I could take it all back," she whispered. "I hate that I let my insecurities get to me like that."

He shook his head. "I should have realized why you'd done what you'd done. I *did* after I cooled off. No man had ever proven to you he was deserving of your trust. *I* was still hedging my bets by offering you a no-strings-attached relationship when I knew how I felt about you."

"About that," she said, her heart swelling as she lifted her fingertips to trace the hard line of his jaw because she couldn't resist the need to touch him any longer, "how can you be in love with me when you called it a fantasy that doesn't really exist that night at the opera?"

"Because you challenge every belief I've ever had about myself and what I'm capable of," he said huskily. "I've been walking around half-alive for a long time, Chiara. Think-ing I was happy—telling myself I didn't need anyone. Until you walked into my life and showed me what I was miss-ing. In *every* aspect."

She melted into him then, unable to help herself, her fingers tangling in his hair to bring his head down to hers. "I love you," she murmured against his mouth.

Passionate, perfect, the kiss was so all consuming nei-ther of them noticed Claudio ambling past them into the café, a newspaper tucked under his arm. "Took you two long enough," he muttered. "I really don't get modern court-ship at all."

EPILOGUE

NICO DI FIORE MARRIED Chloe Russo in a simple, elegant ceremony at the majestic, storied St. Patrick's Cathedral on Christmas Eve in Manhattan. Dubbed one of the must-attend society events of the season, the nuptials drew guests from around the globe, including many of the famous personalities who represented the face of the Evolution brand.

Chloe, who had chosen the date because Christmas Eve had been her father's favorite night of the year, walked down the aisle in a showstopping, tulip-shaped, ivory Amsale gown which left an inspired Chiara dying for a sketchpad and pencil, dress designs dancing in her head.

The five hundred guests in attendance remarked on Chloe's serene, Grace Kelly–like beauty and timeless elegance. *A dark-haired version*, they qualified. Mireille, who preceded Chloe down the aisle in a bronze gown that matched the glittering metallic theme of the wedding, was her blonde equivalent.

Nico looked devastating in black Armani, as did his two groomsmen, Lazzero and Santo, whom Samara Jones cheekily underscored from her position in the gallery, had been on her summer must-have list. Humor, however, gave way to high emotion when Chloe began to cry the moment she reached Nico's side, overcome by the significance of the evening. Nico held her until she stopped, which hadn't left a dry eye in the house.

Then it was off to the magnificent Great Hall of the Metropolitan Museum of Art in Central Park for the lavish dinner reception and dance. With its immense domes, dramatic arches and marbled mosaic floor, it was suitably glamorous for the sophisticated crowd in attendance.

Chloe had wanted it to be a party, for the guests to dance the night away and celebrate. Which it surely was. As soon as dinner was over, the lights were dimmed to a sparkling gold, and the festivities began with the bride and groom's first dance to Etta James's "At Last," sung by LaShaunta, the famous pop star who fronted Chloe's wildly popular perfume Be.

Chiara found herself caught up in the romantic perfection of it all. With Lazzero consumed by his best man duties, she danced with partner after partner as the live band played. But all night long, she felt his gaze on her in the shimmering, sequined, off-the-shoulder dress she'd chosen especially for him, its glittering latte color somehow apropos.

Mireille, Chloe's sophisticated, irreverent sister she was growing to love, gave Chiara an amused glance after one such scorching look as they stood on the side of the dance floor, recovering with a glass of vintage champagne. "He's so crazy about you, he doesn't know which way is north and which way is south."

Chiara's heartbeat accelerated under the heat of that look. She knew the feeling. And it wasn't getting any more manageable, it was only getting worse, because Lazzero had been there for her every step of the way as she'd taken on the coveted incubator position with Bianca and worked to prove herself amidst so much amazing talent. Through her decision to go back to school. He'd come to mean so much to her, she couldn't actually articulate it in words.

"I never thought I'd see it," Mireille mused. "The Di Fiore brothers fall. Nico, I get. He was always the nurturer and he was always in love with Chloe. But Lazzero? I thought he was *untakeable*. Until I saw him with you."

So had she. Her gaze drifted to Santo, entertaining a bevvy of beauties on the far side of the dance floor. "What about Santo? Do you think he'll ever commit?"

A funny look crossed Mireille's face. "I don't know. There was a girl…a long time ago. Santo was madly in love with her. I think she broke his heart."

Chiara rested her champagne glass against her chin, intrigued. "Is there any chance they'll get back together?"

"I would say that's highly unlikely."

She was about to ask why when Mireille, clearly deciding she'd revealed too much, changed the subject. "Your dress is amazing. Is it one of yours?"

Chiara nodded.

"I need one for Evolution's Valentine's event." Mireille tipped her glass at her. "Would you make me something similar?"

"Of course." Chiara was beyond flattered. Mireille was a PR maven, one of the highest-profile socialite personalities in New York. *Everyone* noticed what she was wearing.

She was still bubbling over at the idea when Lazzero came to claim his dance, his official duties over for the evening. The champagne popped and sparkled in her veins as she tipped her head back to look up at him. "Mireille loves my dress. She asked me to make her one for Evolution's Valentine's event. Can you believe it?"

"Yes." He brushed his lips against her temple in a fleeting caress. "The dress is amazing, as are you. Speaking of which," he prompted, "when are you finishing up work at the bakery?"

"Next week. My aunt Gloria called me today to tell me she's retiring. She's going to take on my shifts at the bakery to give herself something to do, which is so perfect," she bubbled, "because my father adores her. It'll be so good for him. Oh," she added, "and the *jaw-dropping* news? My father is playing *briscola* at Frankie DeLucca's house on Friday nights. Can you believe it?"

Lazzero smiled. "Maybe you going to Italy was exactly what he needed."

"Yes," she agreed contemplatively, "I think it was."

She chattered on until it became clear Lazzero wasn't really listening to her, that absentminded look he'd been wearing all night painted across his face.

"Have you heard a word I've said?" she chastised.

"Yes." He shook his head at her reproving look. "No," he admitted. "I need some air," he said abruptly. "Do you need some air?"

She looked at him as if he was mad. It was December and her flimsy dress was not made for this weather. But she knew Lazzero well enough now to know that when he needed to talk, she needed to listen.

They collected their coats and walked hand in hand out into a winter wonderland, Central Park covered in a dusting of snow that made it look as if it had been dipped in icing sugar. It was magical, as if they had the park all to themselves. She was thinking it had been the *perfect* idea, when Lazzero tugged her to a halt in a pretty clearing flanked by snow-covered trees.

She tilted her head back to look up at him. But now he was holding both her hands in his, and she thought she could detect a slight tremor in them, and her heart started to hammer in her chest. "Lazzero," she breathed, closing her fingers tight around his. "What are you doing?"

He rested his forehead against hers for a moment, took a deep breath, then sank down to one knee. Her legs went so weak at the sight of him there, she thought she might join him.

He delved into the inside pocket of his dark suit. Pulled out his fist. Uncurled his fingers. Her breath caught in her chest as the moonlight revealed the magnificent asscher-cut diamond in his palm.

Her ring. The ring she'd dreamed about. The ring she wanted back. Desperately.

Her eyes brimmed with tears that spilled over and ran down her cheeks. A frown of uncertainty crossed Lazzero's face. "You like the ring, don't you? I've been going back and forth all week on it. I thought maybe I should buy you another, but I bought this one for you. Because it reminded me of you. Full of life, vibrant, *impossibly strong.*"

She stifled a sob. *He* made her feel strong. Impenetrable. Bulletproof. As if she could take on the world.

"I love the ring," she managed to choke as she shoved her hand at him. He slid the ring on, the heavy weight of it sliding a piece of her heart back into place.

His face smoothed out. "I'm no Alfredo," he said huskily. "But I want to have that once-in-a-lifetime love with you, Chiara. I want to be the guy who's always there for you. The one who never lets you down. *If* you will do me the honor of becoming my wife."

Her fingers tugged at the lapels of his coat. Rising to his feet, he collected her against him and kissed her until she was breathless. And then buttons on coats were a problem in their haste to get closer to each other. When that proved too frustrating an exercise, Lazzero swung her up into his arms and carried her out of the park.

"You're giving up your job at the café tomorrow," he commanded, lifting his hand to flag a taxi on Fifth Avenue.

"You just want me to make you coffee every morning," she accused, a massive smile on her face.

"Yes," he agreed, his face an arrogant canvas of satisfaction, "I do. But only if it comes with you."

* * * * *

COMING SOON!

We really hope you enjoyed reading this book. If you're looking for more romance, be sure to head to the shops when new books are available on

Thursday 26th July

MILLS & BOON

Coming next month

MARRIAGE MADE IN BLACKMAIL
Michelle Smart

'You want me to move?'

'Yes.'

A gleam pulsed in his eyes. 'Make me.'

Instead of closing her hand into a fist and aiming it at his nose as he deserved, Chloe placed it flat on his cheek.

An unwitting sigh escaped from her lips as she drank in the ruggedly handsome features she had dreamed about for so long. The texture of his skin was so different from her own, smooth but with the bristles of his stubble breaking through...had he not shaved? She had never seen him anything other than clean-shaven.

His face was close enough for her to catch the faint trace of coffee and the more potent scent of his cologne.

Luis was the cause of all this chaos rampaging through her. She hated him so much but the feelings she'd carried for him for all these years were still there, refusing to die, making her doubt herself and what she'd believed to be the truth.

Her lips tingled, yearning to feel his mouth on hers again, all her senses springing to life and waving surrender flags at her.

Just kiss him...

Closing her eyes tightly, Chloe gathered all her wits about her, wriggled out from under him and sat up.

Her lungs didn't want to work properly and she had to force air into them.

She shifted to the side, needing physical distance, suddenly terrified of what would happen if she were to brush against him or touch him in any form again.

Fighting to clear her head of the fog clouding it, she blinked rapidly and said, 'Do I have your word that your feud with Benjamin ends with our marriage?'

Things had gone far enough. It was time to put an end to it.

'*Sí*. Marry me and it ends.'

Continue reading
MARRIAGE MADE IN BLACKMAIL
Michelle Smart

Available next month
www.millsandboon.co.uk

LET'S TALK
Romance

For exclusive extracts, competitions
and special offers, find us online:

f facebook.com/millsandboon

⬚ @millsandboonuk

🐦 @millsandboon

Or get in touch on 0844 844 1351*

For all the latest titles coming soon, visit
millsandboon.co.uk/nextmonth